Asser Levy

The Diary of Asser Levy

The Diary of Asser Levy

First Jewish Citizen of New York

Daniela Weil

PELICAN PUBLISHING
New Orleans 2020

Library of Congress Cataloging-in-Publication Data

Names: Weil, Daniela, author.
Title: The diary of Asser Levy : first Jewish citizen of New York / Daniela Weil.
Description: New Orleans : Pelican Publishing, 2020. | Includes bibliographical references. | Summary: Introduces Asser Levy, a member of the first group of refugee Jews who, fleeing persecution, arrived in America from Brazil in 1654 and began a legal fight for religious and civil rights. Includes historical notes, timeline, and glossary.
Identifiers: LCCN 2019041333 | ISBN 9781455625215 (hardcover) | ISBN 9781455625222 (ebook)
Subjects: LCSH: Levy, Asser—Juvenile fiction. | CYAC: Levy, Asser—Fiction. | Immigrants—Fiction. | Jews—New York (State)—New York—Fiction. | Stuyvesant, Peter, 1592-1672—Fiction. | Diaries—Fiction. | New York (N.Y.)—History—Colonial period, ca. 1600-1775—Fiction.
Classification: LCC PZ7.1.W4313 Di 2020 | DDC [Fic]—dc23
LC record available at https://lccn.loc.gov/2019041333

Back-jacket illustration: Detail from The Dutch Colony of New Amsterdam, *in* American History, *by Arthur C. Perry (New York: American Book, 1913*)

Printed in the United States of America
Published by Pelican Publishing
New Orleans, LA
www.pelicanpub.com

To refugees,
the bravest people in the world

A hallmark of the Dutch success was the statement of religious freedom—or, to be more precise, of freedom of conscience—that was enshrined in the de facto Constitution of 1579, which asserted that "no one shall be persecuted or investigated because of his religion." That declaration was a watershed in human history. It was issued at a time of religious strife in Europe, when intolerance was official policy in England, Spain and elsewhere, when maintaining a state religion was considered a matter of stability and common sense. The Dutch went in precisely the opposite direction and proved that tolerance could actually strengthen a society.

—Russell Shorto, June 2018

Contents

This book is set in OpenDyslexic, a typeface designed against some common symptoms of dyslexia.

Acknowledgments

I want to thank the following people who helped me on what ended up being my own odyssey in writing this book: Toya Dubin, archivist for the New Netherland Institute, for being a mentor and supporter of my project from its early stages and believing in me. My incredibly intelligent aunt Dr. Maria Luiza Tucci-Carneiro, who is a world expert on the history of the Jews in Brazil and from whom I first heard this story. She also happens to curate the Shoah Archive Project in Brazil, www.arqshoah.com. Historians and experts Dr Jaap Jacobs (aka Petrus Stuyvesant!), Dr. Noah Gelfand, Dr. Leo Hershkowitz, Dr. Charles Gehring, Dr. Wim Klooster, Dr. Firth Fabend, Russell Shorto (author of the amazing *The Island at the Center of the World,* a must read!), Len Tantillo and Gordon Miller (historical painters extraordinaire), and Ann Wainer. Zachary Edinger, of Shearith Israel, for giving my family a tour of that synagogue and the Jewish cemetery in Chinatown in the middle of the hottest day of summer. Rabbi David Weitman of the Jewish Immigration Museum in São Paulo for the tour and book. Joel Cahen and Julie-Marthe Cohen from the Jewish Historical Museum in Amsterdam. Dr. Bruno Miranda, who took time to rummage through the Dutch archives in Recife and who answers all my Dutch-Brazil questions on WhatsApp. Jacques Ribenboim, a leader of the Jewish community in Recife, who took my family on an all-day tour of the colonial section, the synagogue, and the possible grounds of the Jewish cemetery. Ton Tielen, archivist for the Dutch West India Company archives in Holland, who finds and translates documents for me at the snap of a finger. Ainsley Cohen Henriques, head of the Jewish community in Jamaica and a direct descendant of one of the characters in the book. Chico and Lea Weil, my parents, who have always supported my career choices. Finally, my husband, Erik, and daughter, Lucy, for five years of putting up with me with my head in the seventeenth century.

Note to readers: Boldfaced words in the diary indicate that a definition may be found in the glossary.

The Diary of Asser Levy

Map of possible route from Recife to New York

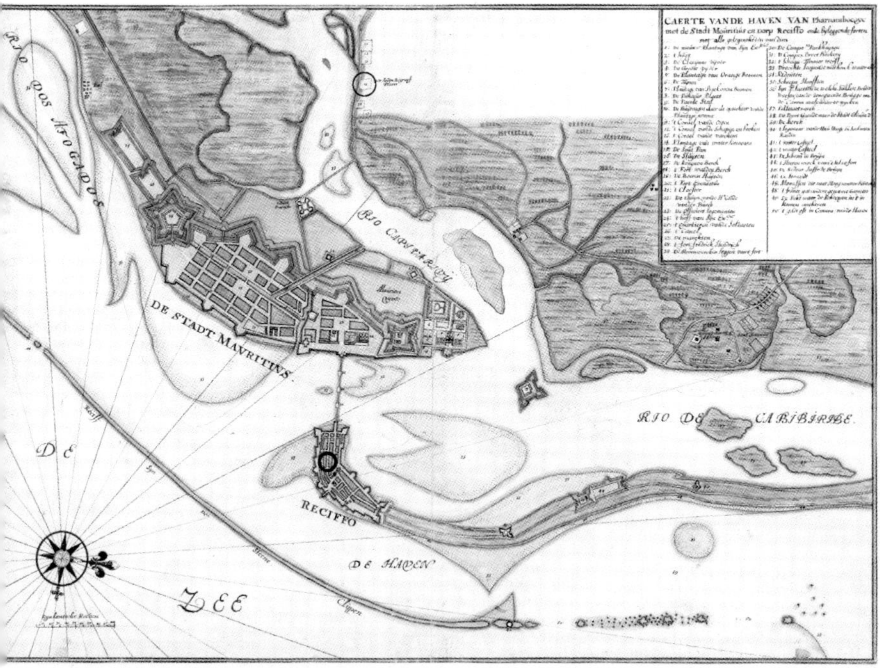

In 1630, the ***Dutch*** *captured part of the Portuguese colony of Brazil. The capital of this colony was Recife (pronounced Heh-SEE-fee). The* ***Dutch West India Company,*** *one of the largest trading companies in the world, recruited people to move to Brazil and run its business there. The Jews in the* ***Netherlands,*** *most of whom had fled Portugal because of the* ***Inquisition,*** *were perfect candidates. They not only spoke Portuguese but were experienced traders and shippers. By the 1640s, close to a thousand Jews had made the journey from* ***Amsterdam*** *to Recife. They made a good living working for the WIC. Dutch Brazil was a religiously tolerant colony. It was considered a "Colonial Jerusalem." The thick circle on the map indicates the approximate location of Kahal Zur Israel (Rock of Israel), the* ***synagogue.*** *The thin circle indicates the Jewish cemetery.*

This diary belongs to Asser Levy.
If found, please return to:
Street of the Jews #36
Recife, Pernambuco
Brazil

January 26, 1654

Four days passed since I last heard the deafening blasts of cannon fire. The morning sea breeze no longer carried the acrid, ominous smell of gunpowder. Word around town was that the Dutch would surrender to the Portuguese. I could not believe that. We must fight to the end.

Outside, I heard a shout: *"The agreement has been signed!"*

I should have ignored General von Schkoppe when he ordered me to take a break from fighting alongside the Dutch Resistance. "You're a young lad," he said. I know I am a teenager, but courage has no age. I should have been protecting my city of Recife all along.

Gen. Francisco Barreto's army had already recaptured most of the Dutch territory. Recife was the last stronghold of the Dutch West India Company in Brazil. Twenty-four years after the Dutch fought to win this territory from the Portuguese, the Portuguese were taking it back.

I stepped onto the balcony. The streets were eerily empty. My father walked up behind me and put his hand on my shoulder. "Son . . . ," he began. I turned around.

"Tahte . . . ," I muttered.

Father looked me sternly in the eyes. "Asser, the Portuguese are here. They will come after the Jews. And you? You fought against them. They will punish you!" he cried. He was right.

"Everything will work out," I pretended to comfort him, and myself.

This afternoon, General Barreto summoned the citizens to the Dutch fort for an announcement. Hundreds of us walked under the blistering sun, seeking shelter in the cool shade of the now powerless tall stone wall. Portuguese soldiers menacingly aimed their weapons at us. The Portuguese general whom the Dutch had fought so hard to defeat now held our lives in his hands.

"The Dutch have waged war against the crown of Portugal," Barreto proclaimed, "yet we shall not retaliate. I will give all foreigners a period of three months to leave Brazil. You may take back any possessions you can carry. We shall provide additional ships needed to return you to your homeland."

A roar of excitement greeted the announcement. I was surprised that the general took pity upon us, since he could have easily killed us all. I hugged my father.

"You see, Tahte. I told you everything would work out!"

But he was not convinced.

"Don't count your blessings so soon," he

warned. "When the Catholic clergy arrive, the Inquisition will come for the Jews again. We need to leave Brazil as soon as possible."

February 10, 1654

These last few days have been so hectic. Father and I were packing our things when someone began pounding on the front door. Father cautiously opened it just a sliver, but the Portuguese man outside pushed it open. He forced his way in, saying he was claiming our home in a few weeks.

"Not if I can help it!" I yelled, as I pushed him back out and slammed and locked the door. I would not allow these men to just come in and take our home and this wonderful butcher shop, which had served the Jewish community for so long.

"Son, there is nothing we can do. We must leave. The soldiers will take everything—homes, businesses, sugarcane farms. There will be no use for a **kosher** butcher shop anyway, since there will be no more Jews under Portuguese rule." Though I was raging inside, I knew he was right.

Later, I walked down the Street of the Jews towards the synagogue. It looked like all the other two-story townhouses beside it, but this building was the pride of my town. Every one of its bricks was put in place by my determined Jewish community. Before Kahal Zur Israel, none of the Jews had worshipped at a real synagogue.

I stepped into its dimly lit sanctuary,

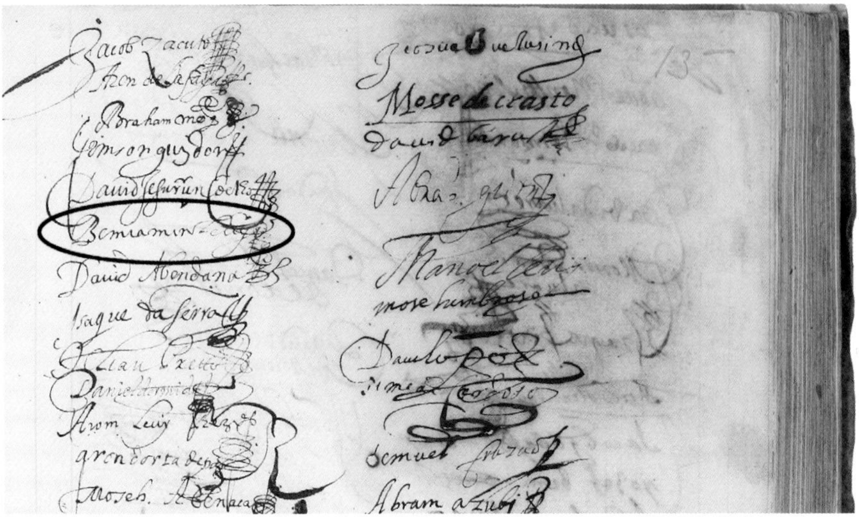

Page from minutes of Kahal Zur Israel synagogue, with name of Benjamin Levy (the kosher butcher) circled (Amsterdam City Archives)

where rows of solid-wood benches faced the raised altar. **Rabbi** Aboab carefully packed the **Torah** scrolls for their long journey back.

"May I help you, Rabbi?" I asked.

He turned his solemn face towards me. "Asser, come here, my lad."

I could barely see his mouth moving beneath the long, thick, white beard. But I could see the tears rolling down his wrinkly cheeks.

"You arrived in this town just a boy, less than ten years ago. I was so proud of you when you stood right here for your **bar mitzvah.** I watched you grow into the brave young man you are now. But soon all of this will be gone, you know. The Portuguese will destroy this building!" he cried, as if already witnessing the men storming in with their sledgehammers.

"I know. But we will rebuild the synagogue elsewhere," I said.

"You will have to fight for that," the rabbi answered. "It's not so easy to build a synagogue in Europe these days."

"I am good at fighting, Rabbi. I will do it."

"From your mouth to God's ears," he said.

Isaac Aboab da Fonseca was the first rabbi in the New World. He was born in Portugal in 1605, and his family fled to Holland during the Inquisition. He emigrated from Holland in 1642 to serve the Kahal Zur Israel congregation. After the Portuguese took over Recife, he returned safely to Amsterdam and continued being a rabbi until his death in 1693. (Etching, 1686, Museum of Jewish History [Joods Historisch Museum], Amsterdam)

Kahal Zur Israel, on Rua do Bom Jesus (formerly Rua dos Judeus or Street of the Jews) in Recife, Brazil, is the oldest remaining Jewish synagogue in the Americas. Dutch-Portuguese Jews established the congregation in 1636. (Photograph by Daniela Weil)

February 12, 1654

At the dock, hundreds of people moved frantically in every direction along the row of ships. They walked in and out of the vessels, carrying boxes and barrels on their shoulders, like hordes of ants chaotically moving around a forest floor. A ship began to slowly pull away from the dock, its deck crowded with passengers.

Finding a ship back to Amsterdam was nearly impossible. I needed to make sure Father could leave safely. I squeezed through the crowd and found the captain of a **caravel.** He was too busy to give a teenager such as me any attention. But I had come prepared. When I showed him my bag of coins (which I had worked hard to earn), and the cage with some of the chickens from the butcher shop, he suddenly seemed interested in dealing with me.

"Tahte, I found a spot for you on a caravel!" I announced with joy when I got home.

Father did not seem so pleased. "But son, what about you?"

"I will be right behind you, Tahte. When you arrive in Europe, Rachel will be overjoyed to see her father again. Meanwhile, I will help the rabbi leave safely. And perhaps I can sell the butcher shop to help us start over. . . . "

I helped Father pack up the shop. Knives, cleavers, saws, books on Jewish law . . .

Father quietly passed me the contents to place in his trunk. Then he handed me an old, rolled-up leather case. I opened it to reveal a worn set of knives with wooden handles, each carefully tucked into a slot. The word *Levy* was inscribed in each of the dull silver blades.

"Your **Zeide** passed these down to me, and now I give them to you. Promise me that one day you will carry on your family's trade," Father begged.

"God willing, I should become as beloved a **shochet** as you are, Tahte," I promised.

February 13, 1654

This morning, I walked Father to the dock. We pushed our way through the crowds and between the mountains of cargo. When we arrived at his caravel, Father took out his **tallit** and covered my head for a blessing.

"I may not see you for a long time, son. You never know what God's plan is, but you are a born leader. You will do great things," he said proudly, lifting my chin. I did not feel like a great leader now.

He walked up the ramp to the wooden vessel. The massive sails inflated with the morning breeze, and the ship slipped away into the green Atlantic waters. I stood there, alone, waving goodbye for a long time. For a moment, it felt as if the ground was slipping away under my feet. My tough and confident attitude melted into tears that flowed like rivers down my face. I was too sad and scared to pretend to be strong now.

February 23, 1654

I made myself busy for several days. That kept me from worrying about my future. I negotiated with the Portuguese to sell the butcher shop. I also helped Rabbi Aboab set off on his journey back to the Old World. Recife began looking less and less like my town. The Catholic churches were coming alive again. It made me nervous.

It was time to find myself a ship. At the dock, I noticed the *Falcon* getting ready for her voyage. I offered Captain Craeck some of the money I received from the butcher shop. He was rather eager to have me on board.

"I'll take all the strong, young men I can get," he said.

I helped load provisions onto the *Falcon* all day. We will set sail tomorrow. Our voyage to Holland should take a good couple of months. It is time to say goodbye to all the friends I made in Brazil: my Dutch neighbors, my fellow Jews. May we live peacefully in Amsterdam again soon!

February 25, 1654

I boarded the *Falcon*'s solid wooden deck before sunrise yesterday. On my back I carried a small trunk with all my worldly possessions: a couple of shirts and breeches, white socks, a hat, a belt, one pair of boots, and a jacket. I also packed my Jewish prayer book, a bag of coins, two candleholders, and the set of knives Father gave me. Then I stepped below deck to claim my hammock. I will be sleeping in a crammed, dark space, amidst cannons and cargo, with my fellow passengers for the next couple of months.

There are around twenty people, plus the crew. It looks as though most of the passengers are Jews. I know every family from the butcher shop. I hope to find a friend on board, maybe someone close to my age. Mr. and Mrs. Israel were arranging their things on some hammocks. They were longtime clients. They have two daughters: Judith, who was quite young, and Miriam, probably fourteen or fifteen, just a bit younger than me. Miriam wore a blue dress with long white sleeves, and her dark silky hair just barely peeked through from underneath her white headscarf. I have seen Miriam in town a few times but never had the courage to talk to her. I may be brave in many departments—but not so much around girls.

"Asser, are you alone?" called Mr. Israel. "Where is Benjamin?"

"Father left two weeks ago," I answered.

"Come stay with us," he said.

Miriam smiled at me as I put my trunk on the floor by a hammock next to hers. I flashed a shy smile back at her. Later, we walked together up to the deck.

Captain Craeck barked orders and the sailors

climbed atop the masts to unfurl the ship's sails. The giant canvases dropped and swelled as if excited to push forward. The sailors then busied themselves with the riggings and releasing the eager *Falcon* from the dock. Then, the ship glided slowly away from shore.

Miriam stood next to me. "Listen," she said.

From the thick, dark jungle, thousands of birds sang their farewells. As the sun slowly peeked over the Atlantic, a soft golden glow shone on the red roofs of my beloved Recife. The ship sailed past **Nassau**'s bridge and along the narrow, rocky reef. Soon, the palm-tree-lined coast disappeared into the sea mist. As we reached the open ocean, a fair, warm breeze whispered in my ear, *"It's a perfect day to sail."*

Miriam must have noticed the grin on my face. "Aren't you scared?" she asked.

"Of course," I answered. "But I am praying for a safe and uneventful journey back to the Old World."

"Same here," she said.

But honestly, I felt a tinge of excitement as a sense of adventure bloomed in my chest.

February 26, 1654

The first night out at sea was quite rough. Mr. and Mrs. Nunes's hammocks rocked next to mine. Mrs. Nunes slept with her newborn tucked away between folds of fabric. The baby cried through the night. I felt both annoyed and sorry for the desperate mother and child. Most people were already seasick at this point. Judith de Mereda was heaving into a bucket all night. She did not look so good. Neither did Mr. Ambrosius.

This morning, I brought water to the passengers who were too sick to fend for themselves. Then, I went up on deck to get some fresh air. Rev. Johannes Polhemius leaned over the handrail, looking out at the ocean. He looked solemn in his long black robe and white neckband, whispering something at the horizon, maybe a prayer. The pastor was probably the only Protestant on the boat, aside from the captain and crew.

"Are you all right, Reverend?" I asked, concerned.

"Yes, son," he answered. "Just praying that my wife and children make it back to Amsterdam safely. We shall be reunited soon, God willing." I knew what he meant and thought about Father, who was probably just beyond the horizon, thinking about me.

"God willing," I replied.

We belonged to different faiths, the reverend and me. He was **Dutch Reformed;** I was Jewish. Under Dutch rule, we all got along. We both knew that we prayed to the same God and that God would find a path for everyone to start a wonderful new life.

March 14, 1654

The *Falcon* has been at sea for more than two weeks. Outside, every day looks about the

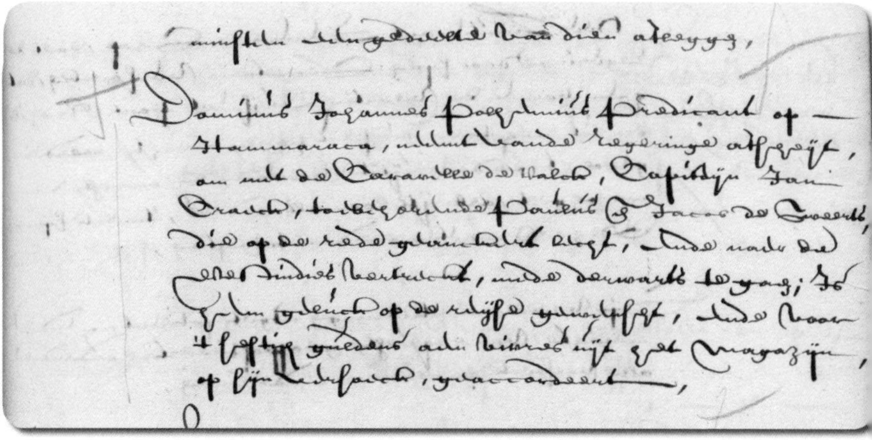

Rev. Johannes Polhemius was the Dutch Reformed preacher on the Island of Itamaraca (pronounced Ee-tah-mah-rah-CAH), near Recife, Brazil, from 1638 to 1654. In February of that year, he boarded the Falcon *alongside the Jewish passengers. After arriving in New Amsterdam, he became the minister of the first Protestant church on Long Island. The minutes of the High and Secret Councils of Brazil, Governor and Councils of Brazil, and High Government of Brazil, shown here, recorded: "Dominus Johannes Pollhemius, preacher at Itamaraca . . . , on board the caravel* The Valck (Falcon), *Captain Jan Craeck, belonging to Paulus and Jacob de Sweerts . . . headed to the* ***West Indies*** *. . . 24 February, 1654."*

same: deep, dark ocean as far as the eye can see, blue skies, moderate winds. Inside the belly of the ship, time passes very slowly.

The long journey is hard on everyone, especially the children. They are bored and have little room to run around.

"Uncle Levy," one said to me. "Can you tell us some stories about the butcher shop?"

"Yes, make it gory," said another.

Not wanting to give them nightmares, I

told them of the time a chicken escaped and ran into the neighbor's house, causing a great commotion. I rewarded their laughter with a sliver of salted meat that I had prepared myself. Miriam, who watched from close by, laughed. Her smile made me forget where I was for a second.

The captain informed us that we were headed towards the island of Martinique. The transition from the blue Atlantic to the turquoise Caribbean was remarkable. It was hard to believe the rumors that these serene waters could be infested with pirates.

As I stood under the billowed sails, the cool breeze hit my face. The sea mist smelled so salty I could almost taste it. I stretched out my arms, feeling energized. Maybe this is why the crew always sings as they dangle from the tall masts. I get a sense of courage and adventure out here in the middle of the ocean. I wonder if this is how Columbus felt just before he discovered the Americas, right around this area. . . .

March 20, 1654

This morning, the *Falcon* rocked harder than usual. I fumbled my way up to the deck to see what was going on. An ominous grey sky had replaced the blue, and strong winds howled. Ripples turned into waves, and waves into giant swells. The captain ordered all passengers to take cover below. Lightning exploded over the ship. The *Falcon* was being tossed around like a toy boat.

Below deck, everyone held tightly to ropes and posts, trying to keep a steady footing. Barrels flew across the cabin, smashing against the walls. I crouched next to Miriam, using my body to shield her from harm. The roar of angry water muffled the frantic yelps above as the crew desperately tried to control the ship.

Hours passed, and the winds calmed.

"Thank you for helping me," Miriam said.

I smiled at her, no longer shy to be her friend. Her family huddled together and held me close as well.

The *Falcon* was finally still enough that I could make my way back up on deck. Miriam followed me. A ray of light beamed through the clouds onto a spot of wrinkled water near the ship. It was surprisingly peaceful outside.

Detail from Ships in Distress Off a Rocky Coast *by Ludolf Backhuysen, 1667* (Ailsa Mellon Bruce Fund, photograph by Daniela Weil)

"Look!" Miriam said, pointing up towards the masts. The caravel's sails were torn to pieces and fluttered limply in the breeze.

This mighty bird had lost its wings. The *Falcon* was adrift.

March 25, 1654

Since the storm blew us off course, arriving in Amsterdam is no longer a goal. We just want to survive. Captain Craeck and crew worked tirelessly to mend the torn sails and broken masts. The barrelmen at the crow's nest kept a lookout for ships or land from sunrise to sunset. I was beginning to think we would be lost at sea forever, until the yelp "Ship!" dropped from the heavens and excitement spread like fire on deck.

The captain grabbed his spyglass to confirm the sighting. But as I stared at the tiny black spot on the horizon, another holler fell like a cannonball onto the ship: **"Red flag!"** Pirates!

"Everyone take cover!" yelled the captain.

I grabbed Miriam's hand and ran below deck. We hid in a corner near our hammocks with the rest of her family. Cannon fire blasted through the air, followed by frenzied stomping above. Unfamiliar voices and laughter became louder as heavy footsteps clunked down the ladder.

Fumbling to my trunk, I reached inside for the leather knife case. I stuffed it inside the leg of my pants, my most prized possession hidden from sight. With a knife handy, I was ready to defend myself and my friends. I had been in battles before and knew what to do. I returned to the corner and crouched with the Israels. Miriam sat next to me; I could feel her shivering. Several raggedly dressed men began rummaging through boxes and trunks.

At the far end of the cabin, a pirate hovered over the crouching crowd.

"*Allez, allez!*" he yelled most of the time. I spoke enough French to understand he was in a hurry. The rest of his words were obscenities.

The tall man slowly made his way closer to us. A large black hat cast a shadow over his face, but I could just make out his menacing eyes. His long beard was woven into a braid, and he smelled as awful as he looked. The pirate bent down and ripped the necklace off Mrs. Nunes's chest. Then he moved over to Mrs. de Mereda and pulled a ring off her finger. Her husband clutched his watch pointlessly. Some of the women began removing pins from their dresses to keep them from being torn. I held my breath and reached for the knife.

The pirate approached us. I gripped my knife. Suddenly, a command came from the deck, and the filthy men stomped back upstairs. Were they leaving the ship already? We remained tucked away for what felt like hours, until we could no longer hear the pirates' gruff voices.

When it was clear that they had left, people began to timidly crawl out of their hiding spots and check on each other.

"I will go see what's going on upstairs," I proclaimed.

"No, Asser, it may not be safe yet," whispered Mr. Israel. His daughter's face reflected his concern.

"Don't worry—I'll be fine," I assured them, running off towards the stairs. I eagerly climbed the ladder and peeked outside. Ragged sails dangled on broken masts. Ropes lay on the deck like dead serpents. The pirates had completely ransacked the cargo and taken much of the food and water. But it appeared that we were all safe.

March 27, 1654

For the next couple of days, the crew continued to repair the *Falcon.* Her timbers creak as she limps aimlessly under the burning Caribbean sun. There is shade below deck, but the ship is now unkempt, and the foul smell keeps everyone outside. At least there is some fresh air there. Drinkable water is mostly gone. My dry throat burns. We give any crumbs or stale biscuits to the starving children.

I try to protect myself from the sun by crawling into the shifting shade of one of the torn sails. Today Miriam sat beside me. Occasionally, we glanced at each other, hopelessly. We had little to say and no energy to speak anyway.

A yelp from the crow's nest broke the silence: "Land ho!"

April 1, 1654

It was a miracle to set foot in Jamaica. I was so happy that I knelt, kissed the soil, and thanked God for saving our lives. Port Royal bustled with energy. People of all types swarmed the dock, which was piled with boxes and goods. Soon, some Spanish guards walked towards us. Noticing our condition, they brought us water. I do not remember a better feeling than pouring crisp, clean water onto a bone-dry throat.

Captain Craeck warned the passengers and crew to stick together. He had been to this island before and was not convinced we'd be safe. There were indeed some shady characters about, making it look as though we had landed in pirate headquarters.

The guards approached Captain Craeck. I could understand most of what they said, since Spanish is quite like Portuguese.

"Port of origin?" they asked.

"Recife, Brazil," answered the captain.

"Your passengers are Portuguese?"

"We are employees of the Dutch West India Company, sir. The Portuguese crown has expelled us. We are on our way back to Holland."

"Oh, Protestants and Jews then? You know Jamaica answers to the Catholic Church?" the guards inquired.

Captain Craeck chose not to reply further. He knew that trouble was brewing.

"Passengers of the *Falcon!*" bellowed a

guard. "Your landing in Spanish territory is most unfortunate for you. You will be interviewed by the Tribunal of the Holy Office of the Inquisition, which will determine if you have committed the crime of heresy against the Catholic Church. Follow me."

April 2, 1654

What happened next, I couldn't have imagined in my worst nightmare. Several guards rounded up the Jews and marched us into Spanish Town. I stuck by Miriam's side, determined to protect her from these dangerous men. We entered a small church.

"Women and children on one side, men on the other," yelled a guard.

"I'm staying with her!" I objected.

The guard pushed me away. I felt powerless. I watched in anger as Miriam, her sister, and mother walked towards the other side of the room.

The men were taken into a small cell behind the church. The room was dark and damp. The foul smell of urine made me gag. From a tiny window high up near the ceiling, just enough light came in to show the worried expression on the men's faces. Mr. Israel paced back and forth. All these men's families had escaped from Spain or Portugal to Holland many years ago. They may have been forced to convert to Catholicism before they left. Once they arrived in Holland, they had been free to practice Judaism again. In a Spanish territory, practicing Judaism as a Catholic convert is a crime punishable by death.

"We shall begin the inquiries," the priest announced. "If any evidence of heresy is found, you will remain in custody and await deportation to Spain."

Ships and Landscape at Port Royal, Jamaica, *from* A Picturesque Tour of the Island of Jamaica, *by James Hakewill (1825). Christopher Columbus conquered Jamaica in 1494. It was loosely ruled by his descendants and a handful of powerful Spaniards and clergy. When the* Falcon *arrived, many secret Jews probably lived in Jamaica, having fled Spain to avoid the Inquisition. Most of them had likely converted to Christianity at some point in Spain but, far from Europe, were secretly practicing Judaism on the island. However, the authorities could not ignore the arrival of a ship full of Jews from the Dutch colony. Their arrest surely concerned the local Jews. Some scholars believe that those same Jews may have helped the British take over the island from Spain the very next year.*

April 10, 1654

The questioning has been grueling for more than a week. The men are taken in, one by one, to speak to the Inquisitor. I have been interrogated several times. Each time I am asked the same questions and give the same answers.

I was born in the German region.

I moved to Amsterdam when I was young.

My father's name is Benjamin; he is a butcher. We moved to Recife in 1648.

My mother, God bless her soul, is deceased.

My sister, Rachel, is in Amsterdam, I presume.

I have never set foot in Portugal or Spain or any country under the influence of the Catholic Church, before now.

I have never converted to Catholicism nor been a Christian. I have been a Jew my whole life, so I could not be a **heretic.**

Yiddish is my first language, but I speak German, Polish, Portuguese, Dutch, and some French.

As far as I know, the adult Jews on the ship were all born in Holland. They have always been Jews.

You must let us all go because we are Dutch citizens and you have no right to imprison us under the peace treaty signed between the Netherlands and the king of Spain!

The Inquisitor dips his quill into his jar of black ink and writes everything I say in a huge, thick book. And then I get thrown back into a solitary cell.

I am hungry. I have no energy, yet I cannot sleep at night. I wonder how Miriam is doing. I wonder if my father is in Amsterdam yet. I wonder if I will live to keep my promise to him to carry on our family's trade.

April 24, 1654

A soft beam of light shone on the wall where I had been marking the days since I was thrown into this cell. As I began to scratch a new line for day fourteen, the cell door banged open. The Inquisitor sternly stared at me.

"Asser Levy," he said. "Follow me."

He led me into the Inquisition room.

"Mr. Levy, I have found no evidence in the records that you have ever converted to Christianity. Your family arrived in Holland from Northern Europe and not Portugal, like the others on your ship. You are a Jew and your soul will not be saved. But you are not a heretic. You are free to go. Please find a way to leave this island as soon as you can."

Freedom gave me a burst of energy, and I ran out of the church. Blinded by the strong sunlight, I stumbled into the town square.

I asked everyone I encountered if they had seen a girl, giving them a description of Miriam's stature and dress. Finally, someone pointed me in the direction of her whereabouts.

I knocked on the door of a hut. When it opened, a man's emaciated face peered back at me.

"Miriam, look who is here!" the man yelled.

June 1, 1654

I spent the next several days resting with the Israels and catching up on the news. Most of the ship's passengers had been released by then. But it looks as though the Church has kept Mr. de Mesquita and a few others. I wish I could rescue them, but I can't. The only thing I can do is let the Dutch government know as soon as I can that there are Dutch citizens imprisoned in Jamaica.

Captain Craeck and the crew made sufficient fixes to the *Falcon* to take us out of Jamaica—but not too far. We had to buy provisions for the next leg of our journey.

Today I walked with Miriam to the market. We ate mangos and guavas and filled up a bag for the trip. My coins were spared from the pirate attack, so I purchased some dried meat and biscuits.

June 20, 1654

I never thought I would look forward to boarding the *Falcon* again, but the prospect of leaving Jamaica and getting back home was comforting. I resettled in my hammock next to the Israels and was happy to see that most of the passengers were back to their spots. I counted twenty-three of us, including the children. The reverend made twenty-four.

The journey to **Cuba** was relatively short. Santiago was a busy port, with lots of trading ships coming and going. Here, we hoped to find a ship heading back to Holland.

Captain Craeck needed a group to venture out and look for such a ship but advised that most people stay on board. This was, after all, Spanish territory, and we could once again be in danger. I volunteered to go, along with a couple of other men.

We walked up and down the dock, looking for a ship on the way to Europe. As we passed a **frigate** called *St. Catherine,* I heard a French-speaking crew and sought out their captain. Capt. Jacques de La Motthe, pronounced "Zhok Duh Lah-*Maht,*" was a stately looking man, dressed like a respectable Frenchman—hat, jacket, necktie, and all.

In my rusty French, I explained our situation to the captain. We were desperately looking for a ship back to Holland, probably the only safe place we could land as Jews at this point.

"I'm not heading to Holland, my lad," he apologized. "I am, however, preparing to return to **New France.** I will be passing New Amsterdam, just a dozen leagues or so south of New England. It is a Dutch colony. You will be safe there."

I called over Mr. Israel and Mr. Ambrosius to discuss this possibility. We all agreed that

New Amsterdam sounded like a safe place to go. We told the captain we were interested in his offer.

"Excellent! The journey will cost 100 **guilders** per person," he announced.

"Captain La Motthe, with all due respect, that is too *much!*" I objected.

The captain knew we had no options. His price was absurd, but he was not willing to negotiate and turned away.

"Wait, Captain," I said. "Let us see what we can do."

"What do you mean, Asser?" asked Mr. Israel. "We could never afford this fare. It will take a miracle to come up with 2,300 guilders."

"Then I will perform a miracle," I replied.

I ran back to the *Falcon*. The passengers were eager for news. I told them about the *St. Catherine* and La Motthe's offer. Reverend Polhemius had enough money to pay for his own fare. As for the Jews, I asked them to gather all their coins—maybe if we pooled our money, we would have enough. I went around collecting everyone's coins. We sat at a table and counted them: 933 guilders. Disappointment set in. But I felt there had to be a way. We made note of how much each family had contributed, and I ran back outside.

"Captain La Motthe. My people on the *Falcon* have lived through great adversity. We lost our homes and livelihoods in Recife. We experienced a horrific pirate attack, and from many of us, they stole what little we had left. We survived countless days lost at sea with little food or water. We were imprisoned by the Inquisition. And we are still here!" I announced. "Please allow us to pay you 933 guilders now, as a group. That is almost half of your payment. The governor of New Amsterdam works for the Dutch West India Company, like we all do. He will surely help with the rest of the payment once we arrive. The Jewish community of New Amsterdam will help as well, you can be sure of it. Do we have a deal?"

"I will take you all for 2,300 guilders. You shall pay me the balance in New Amsterdam," he said.

"Deal!" I said. We shook hands.

"Mazel tov," shouted my friends. "You have really performed a miracle, Asser!"

Finally, our luck appeared to be turning.

August 15, 1654

Before leaving Cuba, Captain La Motthe stopped at Cape St. Anthony for some business. This delayed our journey somewhat, and we were all the more eager to get going. We sailed gingerly through the Old Bahama Channel, an area made treacherous by reefs and shipwrecks. Now we are navigating parallel to the coast of America. Yesterday, we sailed past Delaware. The air here is certainly no longer tropical, and

I had to get my black jacket out of my trunk. I had not felt the chill of a cool evening since my childhood in Europe.

September 5, 1654

This morning, the *St. Catherine* turned and entered a large bay. The ship slipped through a narrow passage between two forested hills. We drifted into calm, sheltered waters, leaving the agitated open ocean behind. In the distance, the tip of an island covered in mist slowly became visible. All the passengers came up on deck to witness the sight.

"Passengers, welcome to the island of Manhattan!" announced La Motthe.

A tall, blurred structure appeared at the tip of the island. As we broke through the fog, its distinct shape came into focus.

"Look, Miriam, a windmill!" I announced to my friend.

She gave me a joyous hug.

At the sight of the Dutch landmark, a wave of relief washed over the passengers. I had not seen smiles on the faces of these families in a long time. The crew dropped anchor before a small village. A row of Dutch-style houses lined the street in front of us. A large fort guarded the bay a little to the west. Well, we were not in Amsterdam, but right now, being in New Amsterdam felt just as good.

There was no dock in town, so a crew member paddled us to shore in small groups. I arrived with the first group and gave a hand to the others as they set foot on Dutch soil once again. Behind us, a rusty, weather-beaten plaque read ***Pearl Street,*** which seemed aptly named given the numerous broken oyster shells covering its surface. The air smelled of a salty mist mixed with the foul odor of an unkempt barn. Pigs and hogs foraged in piles of garbage that were strewn about.

The townsfolk, who had been busy with their morning duties, slowly took notice of the newly docked ship.

"Goedemorgen," they said politely. Yet they could not help staring at us. Indeed, with our dirty, torn, warm-weather garments, we must have looked very much like disheveled paupers from anywhere but Holland. The residents listened attentively as we told them the story of our unfortunate and frightening journey.

Then, everyone dispersed as a serious-looking man made his way through the crowd. Standing authoritatively in front of the group, he cut a larger-than-life figure. A great feather adorned his hat, and he displayed his right wooden leg like a trophy. As he looked us up and down, he could not hide his displeasure.

"I am Petrus Stuyvesant, **director-general** of New Netherland," he proclaimed loudly.

Miriam looked at me nervously, hoping to get some comfort out of my reaction. I was not shaken by his intimidating presence.

Captain La Motthe quickly stepped forward.

"Greetings, sir," he said. "I have brought these passengers from the West Indies. Most of them are Jewish. They have survived a great **odyssey** to arrive at this place. They hope to be welcomed by your Jewish community, who I understand will help pay the balance of their fare to get here."

Stuyvesant laughed vigorously.

"Jewish community? Ha! There is no Jewish community in this town, not if I can help it," he replied. "As for your debt, Captain, I believe you have been tricked."

My heart sank at the announcement of this news. I looked around the crowd of townsfolk to see if anyone might contradict his statement, but no one stepped forward. La Motthe turned and glared at me.

"Jewish community, huh, Mr. Levy? Did you know about this?"

"I had no idea, Captain, I swear. But I promise, the West India Company will help!"

"Well, ladies and gentlemen, until I get my payment, I shall hold on to all your belongings on the ship. And I shall see you in court on Monday morning!"

Reverend Polhemius stepped forward and introduced himself to Stuyvesant. The governor was pleased to see the pastor and shook his hand heartily. Polhemius bade farewell to everyone whom he'd spent the last several months with. He approached me

Petrus (Peter) Stuyvesant (pronounced STY-vuh-suhnt) was the son of a Calvinist minister from the Netherlands. In 1642, the Dutch West India Company appointed him director-general (governor) of the Dutch colony of Curaçao in the West Indies. He attacked the Spanish island of St. Martin in 1644 and was struck in the leg by a cannonball. Doctors in the Netherlands amputated and replaced his leg with a wooden peg. In 1645, after his recovery, the Company appointed him director-general of New Netherland. He served in that post until 1664. Stuyvesant was known for his strong, exuberant personality and his administrative skills. (Image from *Our Greater Country*, by Henry Davenport Northrop, 1901)

and gave me a strong hug. "Good luck to you, Asser. May you be reunited with your family soon."

"Same to you," I answered.

He left alongside the director-general.

I walked towards the Israels. They knew that this was not my fault. Several of the passengers got together to talk about what we would do in court on Monday. We agreed that the Company would come through for us, and we'd be all right. Meanwhile, we borrowed tarps and supplies from helpful citizens, so that we could begin to build tents for tonight.

September 6, 1654

I did not sleep a wink. Though exhausted from months at sea, I could not stop shivering in my tent, which was useless against the cold. I was astonished by such wintry temperatures so early in the year. But at least the sunrise brought the promise of a little warmth.

As I sat on the ground wrapped in my blanket, I heard people approaching the tent. I looked outside and saw two Dutch-looking fellows, properly dressed in black hats, breeches, and leather boots.

"Greetings. My name is Solomon Pietersen," said one of them, in Dutch. "We learned of the arrival of Jews. I am also Jewish."

"I am as well," said the other. "Jacob Barsimon. Nice to make your acquaintance."

I was taken aback. "But I thought there were no Jews here!" I exclaimed.

"We arrived together on the *Pear Tree* about two weeks ago. We came from Holland to try our luck with the beaver trade this winter."

"Mr. Pietersen, Mr. Barsimon, is there any way you can help us, please? We are like chickens, about to be slaughtered."

"Yes, my lad," said Pietersen. "We don't have the money to help you, but I will represent you in court."

During the Middle Ages, the Northern Hemisphere experienced what is known as the Little Ice Age. Peaking in 1650, this climatic change brought with it unusually long and frigid winters, frozen rivers and harbors, and copious amounts of snow. This painting by Thomas Ike depicts the rare event of a frozen River Thames in England in the 1680s. New Amsterdam was also a victim of these bitterly cold winters, and some of its rivers may have similarly frozen over.

I ran to tell the others the wonderful news. We all sat down to talk to Mr. Pietersen. We had to fill him in on the details of our journey and go over the contract we signed with La Motthe, all before tomorrow.

Jacob Barsimon, whose name is also written as Bar Simon, Barsimson, *or* Barsimpson, *is the first known Jew to set foot on Manhattan island. He arrived in New Amsterdam on August 22, 1654. An employee of the Dutch West India Company, he was both a trader and on assignment to scout the possibility of a Jewish settlement in the New Netherland colony. He had been working for the Company in Recife in 1648 so may have known some of the passengers of the* Falcon.

St. Catherine *and* Pear Tree *in New Amsterdam, 1654, by Gordon Miller (2002)*

September 7, 1654

Monday arrived faster than we anticipated. Our weary but proud group strutted down Pearl Street towards the **Stadthuys,** the city hall. It is a large building with typical Dutch **stepped gables**. Its tiled roof supports a steeple, next to which proudly flutters the Dutch flag. Just as we approached, the bell began to ring nine times.

We walked up the stairs and stepped into a large courtroom. As I entered the room, I felt my heart skip a beat. I had never seen a courtroom before. My gaze traveled from corner to corner as I took in the wondrous sight. Leather fire buckets on all the walls hung ready for any calamity. Red cushions lined the seats of the nine councilmembers who would listen to our story, hopefully with open hearts. Near the center of those seats, a tall chair stood like a throne. A tricolor Dutch West India Company flag and fatherland flag hung like tapestries behind the seats. The rest of the room was filled with benches packed with townsfolk, who seemed eager for some entertainment. High above it all was the coat of arms of the city of New Amsterdam, promising to abide by the law of the Dutch Empire.

Our group took a seat on the right, while Captain La Motthe and his crew sat on the left. The council walked in and spread themselves along the front. The director-general limped into the room. Everyone rose as he lowered himself, like a king, onto his "throne." The loud whispers in the room subsided into dead silence.

Captain La Motthe stood and began making his case.

"Your Honor, this group of Jews approached me in the West Indies a couple of months ago. I listened to their tale of misfortune with a kind heart, accepting a payment of less than half the money upfront. They promised to pay me the balance, nearly than 1,400 guilders, upon our arrival in New Amsterdam. I fell for their lies. They never intended to pay me the balance!"

The room filled with loud murmurs from the crowd. I looked around to witness disapproving faces staring us down.

Mr. Pietersen stood to make his case.

"Director-General and Council, these Jews arrived here, like the captain said, in the most unfortunate of circumstances. Like you, they are loyal employees of the West India Company. As we all know, our colony in Brazil was taken over by the Portuguese, and the Dutch were forced to flee. These people paid dearly for the fare to Amsterdam. Sadly, they had the misfortune of being attacked by pirates, lost at sea, and taken prisoner in Jamaica. Captain La Motthe was most kind to save them and allow them to land safely on Dutch soil. The Jews did not lie; they honestly did not know there would be no one to help them here. All we ask the court is for an extension of the payment terms. These Jews are hard workers. They fully intend to pay back the captain's money. Please, consider giving them a little more time. By now, their community in Holland has probably received news of their situation. Perhaps a ship will arrive in due time with money to help them."

At this explanation, the crowd's anger seemed to diminish, and people regarded us with compassion in their eyes.

The councilmembers conferred with each other and the director-general, who stared sternly at us. After some moments, Stuyvesant announced:

"The court has heard both sides of the story. It has decided to grant the Jews a two-day extension for the payment. In the meantime, their belongings shall remain in the captain's custody, aboard the *St. Catherine*. But let me be clear that New Amsterdam does not plan to sustain your penniless group of twenty-three for much longer."

September 8, 1654

I sat by the shore with Miriam as the sun went down. We looked out at the waters of the **North River** as they gently flowed into the **East River** around the fort. Both rivers merged into one large bay right in front of the town.

"I once dreamed the Jews could just arrive in peace and be welcomed and helped,"

I confessed to her. "I never imagined we would become twenty-three isolated **refugees** amongst our own countrymen." I stared at the bay and imagined a large wooden vessel with massive sails, flying a Dutch flag, heroically entering the harbor to help us.

We headed back to the tents. They were nothing more than symbolic shields from the frigid gusts of wind outside. I could hear the children groaning in discomfort all night. And to make matters worse, no ships appeared.

September 9, 1654

Two days have passed since our trial. Today, we had to return to court with Mr. Pietersen and face La Motthe again.

The captain made his case. He had not been paid the remaining guilders. Mr. Pietersen begged for a little more time.

"The Jews have not paid their legal debt to Captain La Motthe," Stuyvesant declared. "However, they have sufficient property on the *St. Catherine*. I will allow the captain to sell all of the Jews' belongings at public auction within four days."

Next to me, Mr. Israel muttered, "How will we make it without our things? How will we survive in the tents without our clothes? We don't even have money!"

It was only September, and the cold was almost unbearable. I heard the locals saying 1654 was going to be one of the coldest winters in history. Most of us had nothing but cotton garments from the tropics. Any trinkets we had left for bartering were on the ship.

I could not answer Mr. Israel's questions. I wanted to leap from my seat and put up a fight. But this wasn't a war. We had lost our case in court. There was nothing I could do.

September 10, 1654

Another frigid night. After sunrise, the Nuneses, Israels, and some other families decided it was time to act. They gathered everyone and told us to follow them to the church, where we would beg for food and shelter.

"What?" I yelled in outrage. "We cannot beg. We are not beggars!"

"What do you suggest, Asser?" Mrs. Nunes replied, holding her baby tightly against her chest.

I had no answer.

The group started walking. I ran after them. Maybe they were right. I had to put away my pride in order to survive.

We all trudged towards the fort. Inside its tall walls was the Dutch Reformed church. Mr. Nunes knocked on the large wooden door. After some moments, it squeaked open, and a pastor peeked out. He was surprised to find, standing outside his church, the group of twenty-three he'd seen in court just yesterday. He looked confused.

"How can I help you?" asked the cloaked man.

"Sir, we have come to ask for your help,"

said Mr. Nunes, filled with shame. "We have no one else to turn to. We are cold and hungry."

"I am **Domine** Megapolensis, pastor of this church," the man said. "Come inside, please."

Megapolensis disappeared into a back room, returning with a bundle of blankets and a few loaves of bread.

We were grateful.

The minister then cleared his throat and herded us back towards the door. "Please understand we cannot provide for you all winter. We do not have the money and have our own people to look after. Have you tried asking the two other Jews in town for help? Perhaps they can assist you." With that, the pastor shut the door behind us.

Later that day, I sat by the water's edge once more. My soul was like the trees, almost bare, with just a few heroic, glowing leaves hanging on. The chilly wind tried to release their grip, and most couldn't hold on. With each leaf that fell, my hope dwindled.

September 12, 1654

Tonight is one of the most important nights of the year for Jews: Rosh Hashanah, the **Jewish New Year.** As the sun disappeared behind the forest, our group gathered at one of the tents. Mr. Pietersen and Mr. Barsimon joined us.

Though we sometimes feel defeated, our strength is in our community. I was so grateful to be part of the **minyan** of ten men chosen to perform the service. We named our congregation Shearith Israel. How fortunate we were that the Israels were inseparable from their prayer book and **shofar,** which we used for the service.

The deep and mournful sound of the ram's horn echoed across the trees and waters of America for the very first time. May it carry our cry for help loud and clear, across the oceans, and towards the heavens.

Shearith Israel, the Spanish and Portuguese Synagogue, is the oldest Jewish congregation in America. It was formed by the twenty-three Jews who arrived in September of 1654. In 1730, the congregation erected a temple on Mill Street (now South William Street), the first structure designed and built to be a synagogue in continental North America. (Illustration by Daniela Weil)

September 13, 1654

As the first rays of light shone over the hills beyond the East River, Captain La Motthe was already busy unloading our belongings from the ship. He lined the harbor with trunks, canvas bags, small objects, books, and some furniture. The auction was to begin early, and the captain looked eager to get it over with.

I walked over to where the Israels were sleeping. I gently whispered into their tent, "It's time." Our whole group of Jews walked together down Pearl Street towards the harbor. We must have looked like a funeral procession. I felt some solace walking next to Miriam.

Pearl Street in the Seventeenth Century, *1901* (The Miriam and Ira D. Wallach Division of Art, Prints and Photographs: Picture Collection, New York Public Library)

The auction was apparently the talk of the town. People left their morning duties and headed for the harbor. I'm sure everyone was eager to see what treasures they could snatch from the Jews. The townsfolk walked around the objects, trying to estimate their value. Occasionally, they glanced at our humiliated faces.

The auction began.

La Motthe opened a trunk.

"We have here one beautiful wooden chest containing some simple yet lovely ladies' and men's garments. One men's shirt, one chemise, one pair of breeches, two nightgowns, two sets of bed linens. We'll start the bid at fifty guilders!"

The villagers alternately whispered to each other and glanced at us, as if seeking any clues as to who may have owned the trunk. A Dutch lady tentatively raised her hand, affirming the starting bid.

"Fantastic!" cried the eager captain. "We have fifty guilders. Who will give me sixty?"

An odd silence followed. Surprisingly, no one made a higher bid. La Motthe pressed on. "Sixty guilders, people—this is a bargain! You cannot purchase garments anywhere at this price. . . . "

More silence.

"Fifty-five guilders, then," he cried in despair.

No hands went up.

Reluctantly, La Motthe yelled, "Sold for fifty guilders."

I could sense the captain's frustration

as he moved on to the second item, a small stack of books. Another offer for the lowest bid, followed by silence. Candleholders, blankets—for item after item, the villagers unexpectedly placed only the smallest possible offers. I turned to Miriam. She looked as perplexed as La Motthe himself.

After the auction, we watched as our property's new owners claimed their things. People grabbed their purchases and began to walk away. But instead of going home, they headed towards us. Each buyer scanned the crowd of Jews, looking for their property's rightful owner. When they found the family, they promptly returned their belongings. We were moved to tears.

Then, I saw a young girl. She held an object I recognized. When our eyes met, the girl walked towards me and handed me the leather knife case. I knelt down and looked into her eyes.

"Thank you," I said. "My father gave me these knives so I could become a butcher. You are so kind to return them to me."

"I hope you become one," the girl replied.

For the first time, I felt that the people of New Amsterdam were my people. Perhaps, this place could be my home. In the distance, I saw La Motthe counting his money, and he did not look happy.

September 16, 1654

The Jews were summoned to court today.

Addressing the council, La Motthe yelled, "The auction was a sham! I barely recouped my losses. I demand the balance of my payment!"

Stuyvesant looked as displeased as La Motthe himself. He was clearly annoyed with the situation.

"Captain La Motthe," he said, "this court agrees that the proceeds of the auction did not amount to the payment of your group's obligation. I order two of the Jews to be put into debtor's prison." He pointed to Mr. Israel and Mr. Ambrosius. "Officers, take these men. They shall be placed in confinement until the debt is cleared."

"No!" yelled Miriam, jumping to her feet. Her little sister cried.

Mrs. Israel hugged her daughters as the men were dragged out of the court into jail. The men protested. They could not believe they were being thrown in jail again.

"Miriam, we will find a way to get the money," I promised her.

"You keep saying that, but it's not true!" Miriam yelled back.

I had to think of something. There had to be a way out of this situation.

I walked out of the court, impatient to discuss the case with Mr. Pietersen. As we stepped out, Stuyvesant approached us.

"You Jews have been a nuisance from the moment you set foot on this land. I have written a letter informing the Company of this regrettable situation. You are refugees and not residents, and I will not allow your group to live and work in my colony. In fact, I will petition the Company for permission to expel all twenty-three of you. New Amsterdam was doing just fine with no Jews around. Good day, gentlemen."

I felt my blood boiling. This seemed like a declaration of war on us Jews. Well, Stuyvesant might have power, but he did not know who he was dealing with. I understood my rights. And now I knew what I had to do.

"Come on, Mr. Pietersen—gather our people. We are going to write a petition of our own."

September 17, 1654

To the Honorable Lords, Directors of the Chartered West India Company, Chamber of the City of Amsterdam.

The Jews of Portuguese origin residing in New Amsterdam respectfully challenge your consideration to deny us the right to remain in New Netherland. That decision will not only be a disadvantage to the Jews, but it will be very damaging to the Company.

Many of us Jews have lost our possessions in Recife, arriving from there in great poverty. We lost the remainder of our possessions during our journey to reach a Dutch colony. As you know, going back to Spain or Portugal was never an option because of the Inquisition.

It is well known to Your Honors that the Jews worked faithfully in Brazil to guard and maintain your colony, risking our own possessions and blood.

New Netherland is an extensive and spacious land. The more loyal people who come to live here and trade, the more taxes the Company will collect. Until now, the Netherlands' government has always protected and considered the Jewish nation to have the same rights as the citizens who live in their colonies.

Your Honors should also consider that Jews are the main shareholders in the Company. They have always taken risks for the growth of the Company.

The Jews in Holland immigrated from their birthplace in Portugal, Spain, and other countries sixty years ago. Many of us were born in Holland and, thus, should have the same rights as other Dutch citizens. We should be allowed to live, travel, and work within the colonies of our new homeland.

Therefore, the petitioners request that you not exclude us but grant the Jews our earned rights to work and reside in New Netherland. Please consider allowing us the liberty to contribute to this town like all the other citizens.

October 26, 1654

Our petition left on the same ship to Holland as Stuyvesant's request. I felt we had made a strong argument, and if the Company was fair, they would take our side. In the meantime, I had to figure out how to pay La Motthe and get the men out of jail.

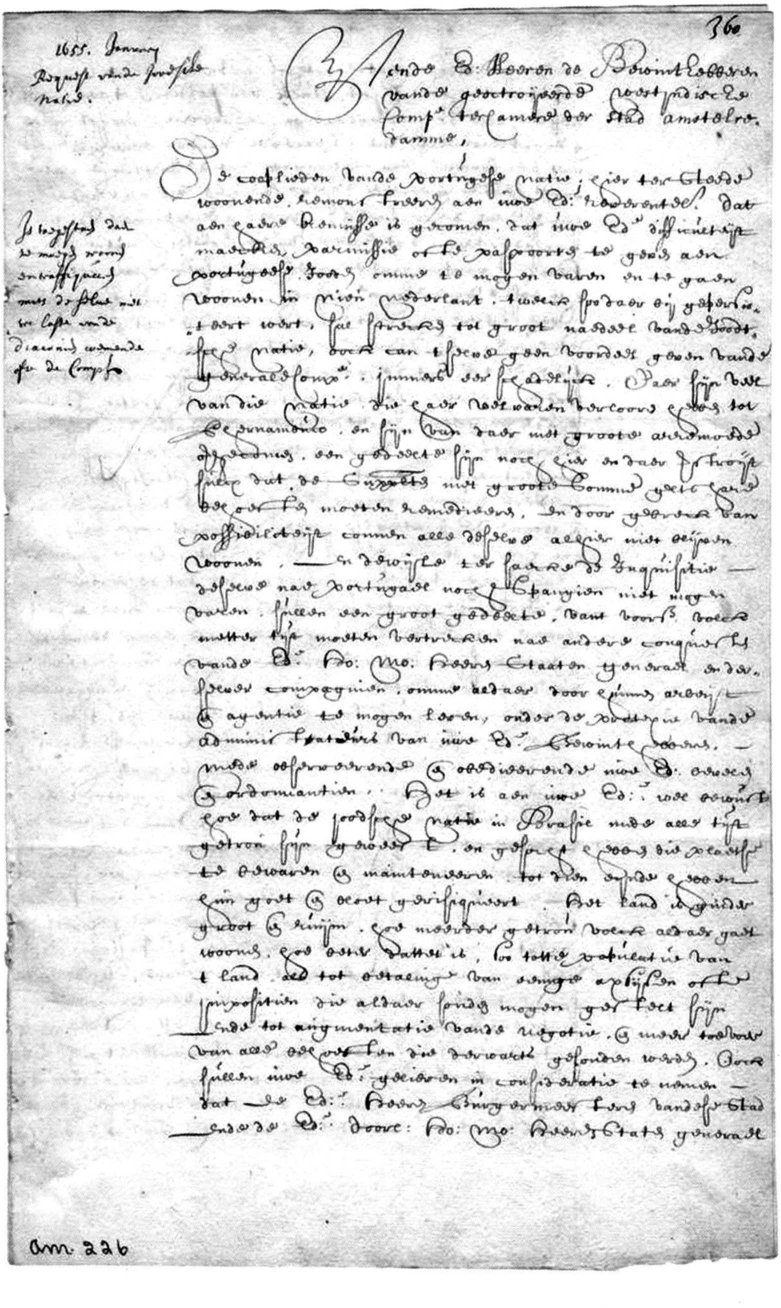

360

1655. January

Aende Ed: Heeren de Bewinthebberen vande geoctroyeerde Westindische Comp.e ter camere der Stad Amstelredamme,

Am 226

Petition of Jews to Dutch West India Company, January 1655 (The Historical Society of Pennsylvania, Philadelphia)

"Pietersen, the situation is getting worse. The captain is relentless. A few weeks ago, he sued me for the 100 guilders for my passage."

"What did the court say?" asked Pietersen.

"They agreed I did not owe the captain anything personally, since he had auctioned off my belongings already," I replied.

"Right . . . 100 guilders per person, 933 guilders paid, nearly 1,400 guilders owed. Property auctioned, two men in jail . . . ," Pietersen murmured to himself.

"That's right," I agreed. "A boat full of Jews, the captain, and his crew, all stuck in New Amsterdam."

"His crew . . . ," he repeated. His eyes widened as if he were seeing for the first time. "How many of them were there?"

"About fifteen, I presume," I answered.

"Has the captain paid them yet?"

"I don't know. But if we stop by the tavern, I'm sure we can find them and ask."

We walked to the tavern. Inside its dark wood interior, daytime turned to night. The air was warmed by the fire and the jolly spirits of the customers. I found a table where several of the crew hunched over their jars of liquor. Pietersen and I pulled up some chairs and sat with them.

"Good morning, lads," said Pietersen. "I imagine that Captain La Motthe has paid you all for your journey here from the West Indies, hasn't he?"

"Nah, sir. He is waiting for the rest of his

payment to pay us," one of them confessed.

"How much does he owe you?" Pietersen asked.

"About one hundred guilders each," another answered.

"That totals about 1,500 for the whole crew," Pietersen calculated, with a grin on his face.

He asked the crew if they would be willing to wait a little longer for their salary, if we paid them their debt with **interest.** They happily agreed.

I knew what this meant. Pietersen and I quickly went to find the captain. He was at the Stadthuys, paying his court fees, which had been mounting up.

"Excuse me, Captain," said Pietersen. "I have an offer for you: would you be willing to transfer your debt to the crew? I understand it's about the same amount of money that the Jews owe you. Your crew has agreed to wait for a ship to come in from Holland with their wages, so long as we pay them with interest."

The captain was taken aback. He reflected on the offer for a moment, then his face lit up. "Yes, I suppose that would work," he answered. "In that case, I will keep the 933 guilders for myself, and the Jews can pay my crew directly. I no longer have to spend my money on these wretched court costs and to maintain the two men in jail. They make me pay for that, you know."

I shook the captain's hand.

"I am sorry for the trouble we caused," I said. "I am glad it's resolved."

"As am I," replied the captain.

And with that, everyone's problems dissolved into thin air. The captain withdrew his suit and released the men from jail. He could then proceed to Canada. And we were finally free.

November 15, 1654

I woke up this morning to find snowflakes floating through the air and landing gently on the ground. I was so excited I barely noticed how cold it really was. I invited Miriam to take a stroll with me through town to admire the wintry scene.

"How is your father feeling?" I asked.

"He is recovering. The days in prison have affected his health. He coughs a lot. But he is quite hopeful that things will get better now. I think we'll stay here for a while," she answered.

We walked by the fort, where the lively sounds of people bartering and selling vegetables, eggs, flour, butter, and chickens filled the market field. No one seemed deterred by the weather. We continued down Bridge Street and walked across the bridge over Prince Canal. The Dutch did not waste any time digging canals wherever they lived, much like in their homeland. The streets were lined with small one-story houses, each with its own little yard. Some were wooden with thatched roofs. Others were stone, with roofs of red clay tiles. Despite the cold, some of the top halves of the homes' Dutch doors were open. The bottoms were always shut, to keep out the pigs in the street. As we walked by, the residents greeted us.

"Good *morning,*" we answered in Dutch. Everyone had a welcoming smile.

New Amsterdam has no huge sugarcane plantations, like in tropical Brazil. Most of the money here comes from the beaver fur trade. People grow their own food and trade some with the natives. They keep animals too, mostly cows, chickens, cocks, pigs, and horses.

We passed a few bakeries. The smell of fresh bread reminded me of Recife. The town is dotted with taverns and breweries. People seem to drink beer like water in New Amsterdam, perhaps because fresh water is rather scarce.

We walked along the bank of the canal, then down Beaver Street. People came and went, carrying buckets of milk and water and logs for their stoves. We can always hear different languages here. These folks had gone to Holland as refugees from different countries, like the Jews. There are Africans here, too, but far fewer than in Brazil. I met many who are freemen and no longer slaves. Even natives from several tribes live amongst us.

Most people are friendly towards the Jews (besides Stuyvesant, of course) and tolerant of our religion. They themselves practice a variety of faiths. I have met Lutherans, Mennonites, Baptists, Quakers, Catholics, and Muslims.

"Isn't it nice," I asked Miriam, "to be in a place where it doesn't matter where you come from, what language you speak, or what you believe in?"

"It is, indeed," she replied.

We walked towards the Stadthuys and stepped inside. I looked at the courtroom, where a couple of months ago all seemed so hopeless. It was empty now. The room looked stately, as if promising justice to all who entered there. Upstairs, I could hear bellows and the thud of a wooden leg against the floor as Stuyvesant stomped across the room.

"So, Asser, what about you?" Miriam asked. "Do you think you'll stay here? Or will you go back to Holland to be with your father?"

"I might just try my luck here," I replied, with a defiant smile.

January 15, 1655

The streets of New Amsterdam are covered by a thick blanket of snow. The sight is no longer as charming to me as it was last fall. Now, it's a constant struggle to keep my toes from freezing.

The trees are bare. It's been a harsh winter. Thankfully, I am renting a small house now. There is nothing much inside it, but it is a house, with a fireplace, a bed, and a roof. That is more than I have had in a long time.

View at New Amsterdam, *by Johannes Vingboons (1665). New Amsterdam in 1654 was a cultural melting pot. Besides the Dutch, colonists came from England, Scotland, France, Belgium, Morocco, Germany, Italy,* ***Bohemia****,* ***Wallonia****, Sweden, Norway, and Denmark. Living side by side with these settlers were also sub-Saharan Africans (both slaves and free) and Native Americans from several tribes (mainly Lenape, Mohawks, and Mahicans). It was said that if you took a stroll in town, you could hear people speaking about eighteen different languages. The official church was Dutch Reformed, but Lutherans, Mennonites, Baptists, Quakers, Catholics, and Jews all coexisted and could worship in their homes. New York's identity as a multicultural city had its origins in New Amsterdam.*

The Jews who arrived here last fall have all found rooms to board in by now. But we are all in desperate need of work to pay for food and rent. Pietersen is excited about the money in beaver pelts. Sailing upriver to trade with the Indians sounds like my kind of adventure. An expedition is about to travel up the North River. But to be able to go, I need a trading permit. That required meeting with an old friend. . . .

I walked to the Stadthuys, going over the speech in my head:

"Good morning, Stuyvesant. I have come to humbly ask for your permission to travel and trade with the ship that is sailing upriver this week. I do believe that I will make a great contribution to the success of the expedition. I promise to proudly contribute to the taxes collected for this colony." I faked a smile as I practiced.

Needless to say, all the rehearsing was for naught.

"Your permit is denied. Neither you nor any Jew shall partake in the colony's business," announced Stuyvesant, with a grin on his face.

"With all due respect, Mr. Director-General," I argued back, "it is our right to live and work in this Dutch colony!"

"Not under my watch," he scoffed. "In fact, the answer from the Company giving me the authority to deport you should be arriving from Amsterdam any day now."

I felt my blood boiling.

"You have no right!" I yelled.

"I have the absolute right, young lad," he snapped. "When I arrived in New Amsterdam seven years ago, this place was in ruins! The Indian attacks were constant; the town was destitute. Almost everyone was gone.

Poor Director Kieft was drowning in problems. I have had to rule this place with an iron fist to put it back in order. I gave up my leg in the Caribbean fighting for the Company, and I will not let a group of penniless Jews bring New Amsterdam down again!" He pounded his wooden leg on the floor. He knew the impact of its sound.

And with that, I realized how hard I would have to fight to remain in this town.

March 20, 1655

Springtime could not arrive soon enough. Ice was melting into water everywhere; even the harbor seemed to be thawing from its frozen winter slumber. A ship finally arrived from Holland. The entire town, anticipating letters and goods from Europe, swarmed the harbor.

Our group of Jews had been eagerly awaiting this ship since September. I ran to Miriam's house, then together we rushed to the harbor.

We watched the new arrivals gather on Pearl Street. Miriam and I walked through the crowd, trying to identify the passengers.

"Listen," she said. "Portuguese!"

We approached a group of men and introduced ourselves. They seemed pleased.

"Ah, Mr. Levy, Miss Israel," said one. "We have heard about you. I am Abraham de Lucena, and these are my colleagues, Mr. Henriques, Mr. D'andrada, Mr. D'acosta, and Mr. de Ferrara. We are Jews, coming from Holland to help."

I all but dragged the newcomers to my home, while Miriam ran to grab her family and the others. After months at sea, the men were happy to stretch out their legs by a fire. As I served them warm soup and bread, I told them about our escape from Recife, La Motthe's lawsuit, and Stuyvesant.

"We have brought money from the community," Mr. de Lucena said. "This should help with your debt. And you should be pleased to know that the Dutch government is negotiating with the king of Spain to get the prisoners in Jamaica released."

"That is wonderful news," I said. "What do you plan to do here?"

"We have heard of how the Jewish community is struggling to gain a footing here. We are respected businessmen in Amsterdam. Hopefully that will help."

"Mr. Levy, I believe I have a letter for you," said Mr. Henriques. He dug through his things and pulled out a sealed paper with my name on it. It was from my sister, Rachel. She said Father arrived safely in Holland. I pressed the letter against my heart and smiled. It felt as though this day could not get any better.

"But wait until you see this," Mr. de Lucena said eagerly, as if saving the biggest surprise for last. He opened a big chest. When I looked inside, my heart filled with joy. It was a Torah scroll.

"A present for your congregation," he said. "May it be around for a long time!"

Several Amsterdam Jews arrived in 1655, shortly after the "twenty-three passengers." Together with Asser Levy, they became the spokespeople for the entire community. They were Jacob Cohen Henriques, Salvador D'andrada, Abraham de Lucena, Joseph D'acosta, and David de Ferrara.

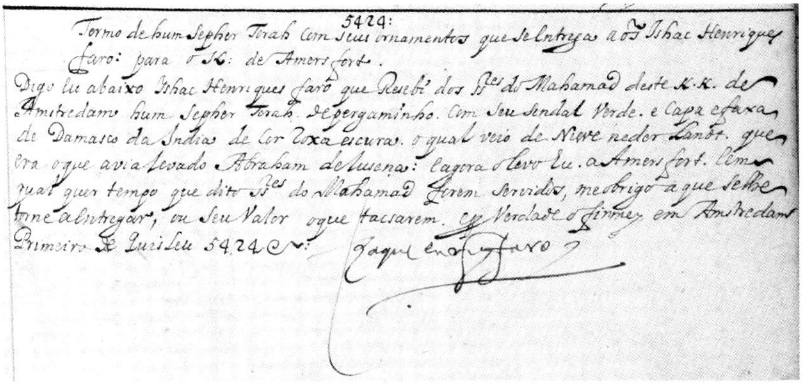

5424:

Termo de hum Sepher Torah Com seus ornamentos que se Entrega a o Sr Ishac Henriques Faro: para o K.K: de Amersfort.

Digo Eu abaixo Ishac Henriques Faro que Resebi dos Sres do Mahamad deste K.K. de Amstredam hum Sepher Torah de pergaminho. Com seu Sendal Verde. e Capa e Faxa de Damasco da Indias de Cor Roxa escuras. o qual veio de Nieve neder Landt. que era o que avia levado Abraham de Lusena: e agora o levo Eu. a Amersfort. Em qual quer tempo que ditos Sres do Mahamad forem servidos, me obrigo a que se lhe torne a Entregar, ou seu Valor o que tacsarem. em Verdade o firmey em Amstredam Primeiro de Quisleu 5424 [illegible]

Ishaque Henriques Faro

Page from Dutch West India Company public archives, showing that Abraham de Lucena arrived in New Amsterdam with the Torah in 1655 (Amsterdam City Archives)

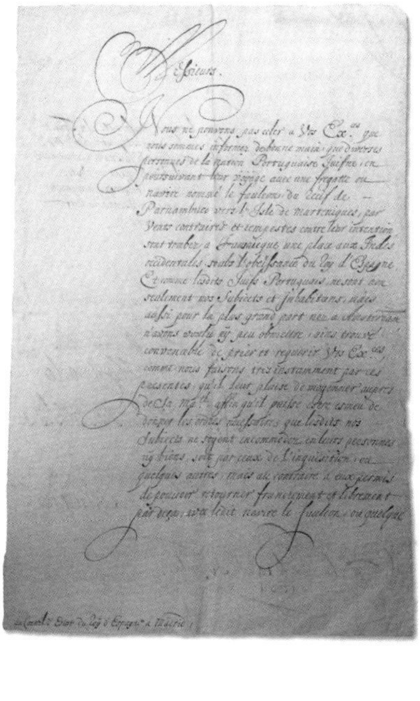

The Dutch government wrote a letter to King Philip IV of Spain in November 1654. In it, they demanded that Spain release the Jews still held captive in Jamaica. They claimed that the Falcon *had unintentionally landed in Jamaica after fleeing Recife.* (Collection of American Jewish Historical Society)

April 10, 1655

Making a living in New Amsterdam has been a struggle. Stuyvesant refuses to allow Jews to trade or open stores. Even our new friends who just arrived from Amsterdam are suffering from his opposition.

I quickly found out that in order to survive, I would have to be creative. My neighbors already knew about my knife skills, so they often called me for butchering services—especially the Jews, since I was the only one around who could give them kosher meat.

I also began to barter with the natives who lived in the area. They were interested in linens, clothing, hats, silver, jewelry, those kinds of things. They paid in **wampum** and tobacco. Sometimes I bartered for food.

Today, I was on my way to pick up some flour at the mill when Pietersen ran up to me, his eyes bright with excitement.

"Asser, have you heard the news?" he asked, out of breath.

"No, what is it?" I couldn't contain my anticipation.

"I have come from the Stadthuys. The letter from the Company—it arrived!" Pietersen proclaimed. He recounted what he had heard:

"It is unreasonable and unfair for you to expel the Portuguese Jews. After reading their petition, we believe they suffered considerable losses in the taking of Brazil. They shall continue working and making money for the

Company in New Amsterdam. The Jews are to be free to travel and trade and to live and remain in New Netherland. This matter is decided and resolved."

We hugged each other, then ran off to spread the news. We had fought for our right to stay and work here, and we won! I could finally go on trading expeditions, and make some money to buy a house, and open my own butcher shop. . . .

As I rushed to Miriam's house, I noticed Stuyvesant coming towards me from the opposite way. He seemed displeased.

"Nice day!" I offered, smiling at him.

"Don't forget, Mr. Levy. Only I can enforce the Company's orders. Or not enforce them . . . " With that, he continued on his way.

August 28, 1655

And so it was. As Stuyvesant was not allowed to officially expel the Jews from his colony, he instead worked hard to make us *want* to leave. Making a living here has been difficult for the Jews. But this month, it seemed that everyone in town had other concerns.

Word had spread like wildfire that Stuyvesant was planning a surprise attack on the colony of **New Sweden** (our neighbors to the south). The Swedes were allies with several native tribes and in direct competition with the Company's beaver trade. Stuyvesant planned to catch them off guard by sailing down the **South River** just before winter. For this, the director-general needed about two hundred strong men. I was eager to join the **trainbands.** Several of the Jewish men and I made our way up **Heere Street** towards the end of town. We arrived at the **Wall.** This fortification kept New Amsterdam safe from any attacks coming from the north. The other sides of the town were shielded by water.

Stuyvesant stood by the main gate of the Wall, facing a line of men who were ready to enlist. He noticed the group of Jews in the crowd.

Section of Wall Street Palisade *(1887). A fortified wall stood at the northern edge of New Amsterdam. It was used to protect the town from Indian raids and a potential British invasion. Today, Wall Street marks the location of this fortification.* (The Miriam and Ira D. Wallach Division of Art, Prints and Photographs: Picture Collection, New York Public Library)

"What are you doing here?" he asked indignantly.

"We are here to enlist for the trainbands," I answered. "We want to serve our town."

"You men do not seem to understand. This line is for New Amsterdam citizens only. You are not allowed to enlist. And besides, these fine Dutch soldiers would not be willing to serve alongside men of the Jewish faith. . . . "

I suddenly felt I was enlisting for the wrong battle. I knew my rights, and I knew that the best place to fight for them would be in court. I grabbed Mr. Barsimon and headed to the Stadthuys. We signed a petition demanding that the Jews be given the right at once to serve in the military in New Amsterdam.

September 21, 1655

Several nights ago, a commotion outside startled me from my sleep. I sat up in bed, waiting to detect another sound but only hearing horses neighing in the distance. Must have been some drunk men leaving the tavern, I thought.

But as I lay back down, a shriek sent shivers down my spine. Something was terribly wrong. I looked out my window and saw fire blazing from a house down the street. Behind it, several pillars of smoke billowed up into the darkness.

Something swooshed through the air, like a small bird but much faster. Then another.

Soon, I realized they were arrows. Knowing I could not fight against a storm of deadly arrows, I took cover under my bed. Hostile natives had invaded. How could that have happened with such a heavily armored Wall? I remembered that Stuyvesant was away with most of the soldiers, not having yet returned from his mission in New Sweden.

Smoke from the street began to seep into my house. I tried to suppress my coughing but couldn't. Outside, pigs squealed and horses neighed so loudly that I could barely make out the cries of women and children in the distance. The frightening howls of the natives were interrupted by occasional gunfire. I remained under the bed for what seemed like an eternity.

By dawn, a deadly silence fell over the town. When I heard the sheriff's voice as he checked on the residents, I felt safe enough to come out.

I opened my front door and stepped outside. My street was unrecognizable. Some houses were scarred from the hellish flames, while others were burned to the ground. Broken furniture and debris littered the street. Chickens fluttered nervously about, and I could make out some dead animals by the side of the road.

I ran to Miriam's house.

"Asser," yelled Miriam, "the natives have kidnapped dozens of people!"

"Is your family all right?" I asked with a gasp.

"Yes, we are all safe, thank God," said Mr. Israel as he approached.

I spent the day helping my neighbors clean up. I offered my house as a haven to a few who were now homeless and needed a place to rest, though I suspected that night no one would dare shut their eyes.

September 25, 1655

Today, news trickled in about what had actually happened. The Susquehannocks had attacked our town. Some other tribes were involved as well. Hundreds of natives had sneaked in during the night from their canoes, just beyond the fort. They had taken more than a hundred hostages. Dozens of homes and farms were destroyed.

When Stuyvesant returned, he walked up and down the streets of his town in disbelief. Crying folk looked to him for comfort, but compassion is not his strength. Stuyvesant never imagined there would be no rejoicing over his capture of Fort Christina from the Swedes. People now were more interested in pointing fingers and finding out who was to blame for this situation.

Word around town was that the attacking tribes had been allies with the Swedes. When Stuyvesant attacked the Swedes, the natives retaliated. But people also whispered about another incident. A couple of weeks ago, a Dutch man shot a native girl in his yard for stealing a peach. The natives had been ready for revenge.

The only person who can resolve this situation is Stuyvesant. Now I will witness what kind of a leader our director-general really is.

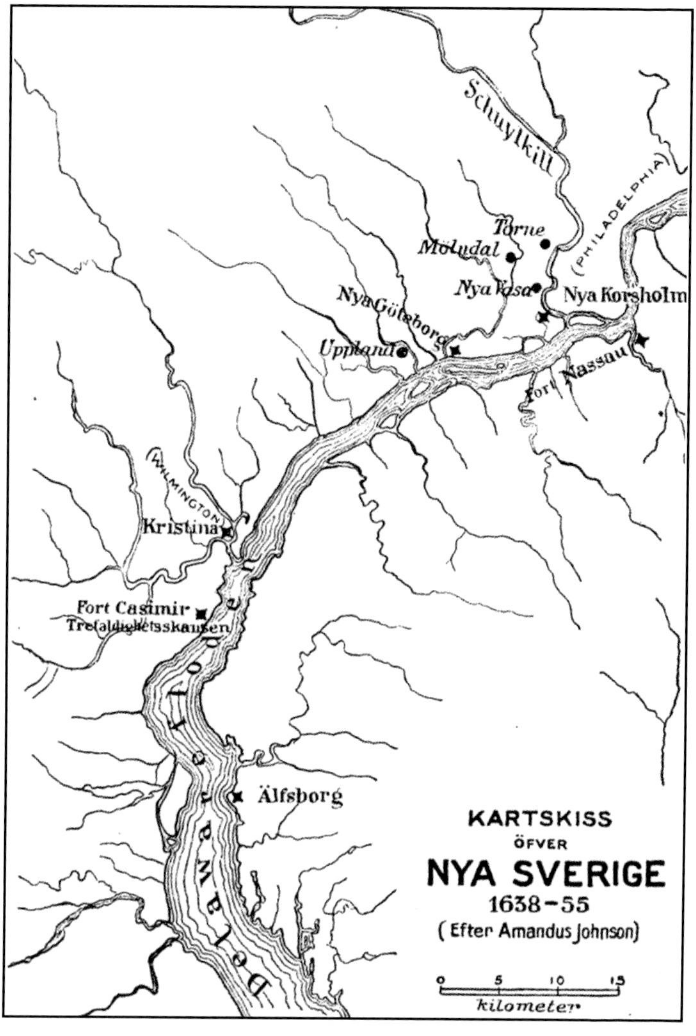

Map showing location of Fort Christina, part of the New Sweden territory on the Delaware or South River, just downstream from Fort Nassau, a Dutch trading post in modern-day New Jersey. In September of 1655, about six hundred Susquehannocks invaded New Amsterdam and surrounding villages in response to a Dutch attack on the Swedes, their allies. The Susquehannocks caused great destruction and took 150 hostages, who were later ransomed by Stuyvesant. As the attack was also possibly spurred by the killing of a young native girl for taking a peach from a Dutch settler's tree, it became known as the Peach Tree War.

October 21, 1655

Since the attack, Stuyvesant has worked very hard to make peace with the natives. He met with the tribal chiefs and signed a new treaty with them. Peace with the Indians is the result of a delicate balance and can tip over at any moment. I applaud the director-general for his attempt at peace. Seeking revenge on the natives will only lead to more bloodshed.

Sadly, Stuyvesant does not show the same tolerance for the Jewish refugees. Our list of challenges grows larger. The Jews cannot own property. We cannot have a store or travel for the beaver trade. We cannot serve in the military (and we are being fined for not serving!). We are refused a plot of land for Jewish burials. The governor has ignored all the rights the Company has given us. And now, after this terrible attack, we are all vulnerable to more.

At this point, most of the Jews have had enough. They want to find a less hostile place to live. I do not blame them.

This afternoon, while I sat with the Israels in their home, Mr. Israel made an announcement.

"Asser, we will be leaving this town."

I looked at Miriam in a shock, and she lowered her eyes to the floor.

"No, Mr. Israel, please stay. Things will get better!"

"I don't believe they will, Asser, but I admire you for staying and putting up a fight," he said.

"Where will you go?" I asked.

"Well, word has it that the town of Newport, New England, has welcomed Jews arriving from the West Indies. We may try that first. The Dutch colonies of Curaçao and Suriname could be interesting too. Moving back to the warmer climate and the sugar business could be a good thing. There is always Amsterdam. . . . "

Miriam gave her father a defiant look, as if she'd argued with him before to no avail. Then the words flowed from my mouth as if they'd always lived there.

"Mr. Israel," I said. "Your daughter has been at my side through thick and thin. I believe I can take good care of her. I would be honored if you gave me your blessing to marry her."

Miriam raised her eyes to me as her face filled with joy. I looked at her mother, father, and sister. They smiled.

October 30, 1655

The ceremony was small and simple. Miriam and I stood under a **chuppah** held by her father, Mr. Pietersen, Mr. Barsimon, and Mr. de Lucena. About ten of the passengers of the *St. Catherine* attended (the rest had departed). Some of my Dutch neighbors also came to celebrate.

Miriam looked lovely, her veil barely obscuring the light in her face. Our friends rejoiced when I stepped on the glass with all my might, shattering it into pieces. I hoped that somehow my father would feel this joy across the oceans. I didn't remember ever being so happy before.

I don't feel like such a "young man" or "lad" anymore. I am somebody's husband. Miriam is no longer under her father's care but *mine*. I must provide for *me* and for *her*. There is no *more* time to waste.

November 15, 1655

The townsfolk have all been working hard to rebuild the homes that were destroyed, before the brutal winter comes again. The Indian attack has cost the Dutch colony a fortune. Beaver-trading season is here. This city needs the money. And God knows I need money too.

It was time to request my trading permits once again. I passed by the homes of the Jewish traders from Amsterdam. We walked together to the Stadthuys, hoping for strength in numbers. Perhaps now, after all the hardship following the attack, Stuyvesant was ready to comply with the Company's orders.

"Your permit is denied!" the director-general stubbornly repeated.

I am more determined than ever to fight for my rights. Stuyvesant is headstrong, but I know the law is on our side. This battle I shall fight without raising a fist. I shall fight it in court.

November 29, 1655

Mr. de Lucena, Mr. Henriques, Mr. D'andrada,

and Mr. de Ferrara all sat around my dining table. We had gathered to write yet another petition to the Company. This was a legal matter that needed to be addressed.

Mr. de Lucena, the most influential of us, had the honor of being the scribe. These black-inked words appeared as his quill danced over the parchment:

Your Honorable Lords, we are gathered to protest for our rights to enjoy the same liberty allowed to other citizens. We wish to not be barred from traveling within the territory to trade, and to be able to purchase our own homes. All of these rights have already been consented to us by you in a previous ruling. . . .

We made it clear that the director-general had not honored the Company's decision.

I took the letter down to the harbor myself. People were busy loading cargo onto a ship that was heading back to Amsterdam. One of my Recife friends, Mr. Ambrosius, was getting ready to board. He said he would be happy to personally deliver the letter to the Company when he arrived.

March 11, 1656

Nights are still rather cold, though it is already mid-March. The fire burning in the fireplace keeps Miriam and me warm at night, but it is constant work to feed it. This morning, I stepped outside to gather some firewood. I inhaled the crisp air. Most of the snow had thawed from the ground, leaving puddles and mud in the streets. I sensed that spring was finally in the air.

I stepped into a wooded area and bent over to collect some fallen branches. Then, I noticed a tiny green bud pushing its way up through the muddy ice. I knelt to study this amazing being, suppressed by months of impossible conditions. I noted its resilient little green leaves, coming to life after a long, cold winter.

I wrapped my bundle of branches and threw it over my shoulder. As I walked back home, I thought about my life and all the hardships I'd endured in the past year. I looked around. Against all odds, I had landed in this place. And by God, against all odds, I would succeed here.

April 2, 1656

The day began like all the other days. Miriam and I shared some bread and butter at breakfast and got ready for our daily duties. Miriam would walk to the market to pick up some milk and food. I would set out to the mill to pick up some flour for baking bread. I had a few butcher visits today as well.

I was grabbing my coat when I heard a knock at the door.

"Mr. Barsimon, good morning," I said, surprised at the early visit.

"Levy, I bumped into Stuyvesant this

morning. He has summoned us to meet at his house," he informed me eagerly.

We gathered the other men and walked towards the harbor. At the water's edge, with a view of the entire bay, stood a three-story stone building. Judith Stuyvesant led us to the backyard, where her husband sat on a bench overlooking a beautiful, manicured garden.

"Good morning, gentlemen," the director-general said, in a more submissive tone than we'd heard before. He was holding a letter. I could only imagine it was the Company's answer to the Jews' petition.

"Good morning, Director-General," we answered politely.

"It has come to my attention that the Company is displeased with how I have handled the situation with the Jewish refugees," he announced. "I have been reprimanded for my intolerance. I am forced to comply with the Company's demands. But first, I would like you to understand my position." He looked at us intently.

"I have a lot on my hands. I have to constantly defend our town from invaders. The British surround us, ready to attack every time I blink. Of course, our relations with the natives are always hanging by a thread. Day in and day out, I have to settle squabbles between our own people," he explained, impatiently.

"Our colony is composed of the most

varied folk, each wanting us to honor their particular customs. The Quakers want to shake. That makes me crazy! The Muslims want to pray on their rugs. We even have to tolerate the Catholics, who killed so many Protestants in our homeland! If that weren't enough, a group of Jews arrived, demanding *their* rights. If I please everyone, who will be next?" Stuyvesant paused, exasperated.

"It is hard for me to know where to draw the line. We are a Dutch Reformed colony. My father was a devout Protestant, as am I. It would have been much easier if everyone here were the same. But we are not. This is the face of the Netherlands, and it is the face of New Netherland. I *must* honor the laws of tolerance that are so important to the Dutch government."

Stuyvesant drew up his chest. "From here on, you will be granted the right to travel and trade with the rest of the Dutch traders. You may buy land or houses. You shall be allowed to own businesses and practice your religion within your homes. The Company wants all religious groups to be granted these rights. I will, as the Company demanded, treat you with respect. But don't ask for too much!"

I looked at the other men, not knowing what to do with all my pent-up emotion. "Thank you, Director-General," we answered, respectfully, as we walked away. As Stuyvesant looked at his well-tended garden, he suddenly did not seem like the same "Petrus" as before.

So much was going through my mind as I stepped out of his home that I could not find the words to speak. My friends probably felt the same, for we all walked back to our homes in complete silence.

When I arrived, Miriam looked at me inquisitively.

"What is wrong, Asser?"

"Sit down, Miriam; I have news . . . " was all I could say.

October 15, 1660

My beloved diary, it has been a few years since I have written in you. My life has been exceedingly busy. I ask for your forgiveness. But today I felt more compelled than ever to write.

It was a beautiful, crisp, fall morning in New Amsterdam. I put on my finest outfit: a black velvet coat, black **waistcoat,** and breeches. I slipped my silver-buckled **pantofles** over my stockings, and Miriam straightened my large, black hat. We walked hand in hand down Pearl Street towards the Stadthuys. I have grown quite accustomed to this walk. I come to court almost daily now, to represent people who need their voices heard, as I once did. But today was no ordinary court day.

I stood up and faced the Dutch council I have come to know so well.

"Council, Director-General, I have come to ask for a special permit today. As you know, I am a butcher and have been serving your community for several years now. My father and grandfather were butchers too. But they were kosher butchers, shochets. Religious law does not allow Jews to eat pork or slaughter hogs. With your permission, I would like to officially serve as my community's shochet."

The council discussed the case with Stuyvesant, who stared at me with piercing eyes. After a few minutes, he stood up.

"The council of New Amsterdam will grant you, Asser Levy, a waiver from having to slaughter hogs. You are free to become a shochet without any concern for being prosecuted on religious grounds."

At that moment, I saw the face of my father as he blessed me in Recife. He held my chin high, and smiled, knowing what potential I had to be a leader. I heard a whisper in my ear, *I am proud of you, son.* I looked Stuyvesant straight in the eye, and he nodded.

Miriam and I stepped outside. She put her arms around me as we looked out at the calm waters of the East River. We stood near the spot where we had landed six years ago. Miriam has been through this whole journey with me and knows what I had to overcome to get to this moment. But only I know how much I still have in me.

Asser Levy

Epilogue

Asser Levy was the first Jew in New Amsterdam to receive the right to travel and trade. He was also the first Jew to be granted **"burgher"** (citizen) rights. When he bought his house on the corner of Stone Street and Mill Lane in 1662, he became the first Jewish homeowner in America. Levy was also the first Jewish butcher in America and opened his own shop near Wall Street and Pearl Street in 1678.

Levy traded in at least nine different kinds of products. He also served as an

Medal created by Alex Shagin in 1999 for the Jewish-American Hall of Fame, commemorating Asser Levy and the first Jews in America (Illustration by Daniela Weil)

attorney and managed people's estates. He traveled upriver to Fort Orange (Albany) and Beverwyck numerous times, where he not only traded furs but also bought and sold property. Acting as an investment banker, Levy lent money to about four hundred different people. He traveled to Holland on business occasionally, perhaps meeting his family there. A Benjamin Levy became the shochet of London in 1664.

Asser Levy house in 1662 (Illustration by Len Tantillo)

In late August 1664, a fleet of English warships surrounded Manhattan, and in a few days, Petrus Stuyvesant surrendered the entire territory of New Netherland to the British crown. Col. Richard Nicolls, the new governor, renamed the colony New York, in honor of the king's brother, the duke of York. In early September, he signed the Articles of the Transfer of New Netherland. This document showed a great appreciation for the government and diversity of the Dutch colony. It allowed all Dutch citizens to remain in their homes, conduct their business as usual, and speak their language. Dutch government officials could remain in their posts (except Stuyvesant). This declaration also granted the following right: "The Dutch here shall enjoy the liberty of their consciences in Divine Worship and church discipline." Colonel Nicolls made sure that New York would adopt the Dutch model of religious tolerance. The petitions and court battles fought by the Jews lived on.

Petrus Stuyvesant, who sailed back to Holland after his defeat, returned to New York a couple of years later, where he lived the rest of his life at his farm in the **Bowery.** He died in 1672 and was buried at the chapel on his estate, where now stands St. Mark's Church in-the-Bowery.

Most of the other passengers of the *St. Catherine* seem to have left the colony. The oldest known Jewish grave in New York today belongs to Benjamin Bueno de Mesquita, who died in 1683. He was a former resident of Recife, Brazil, who is thought to have arrived some years after 1654. Asser Levy seems to be the only one of the original twenty-three who stayed in New York, becoming the first Jewish citizen of New York and possibly America. He continued his activities as a businessman under British rule.

Levy died on February 1, 1682. At the time, he was considered the thirty-eighth wealthiest

Lithograph entitled The Residence of N. W. Stuyvesant *(1857), showing Stuyvesant's house in the Bowery. The word "bowery" comes from the Dutch word* bouwerij *(pronounced BOW-uh-ree), which means farm. There were several farms north of the city's wall, one of them being Petrus Stuyvesant's. He is buried in the crypt of a church known today as St. Mark's, in the area of Manhattan still called the Bowery.* (The Miriam and Ira D. Wallach Division of Art, Prints and Photographs: Print Collection, New York Public Library)

man in New York. He and Miriam did not have any children. His sister, Rachel, who moved to New York a few years before his death, inherited his money. Her son, Simon, carried on the family's legacy as a butcher.

New York City Hall in 1679, formerly the Stadthuys (The Miriam and Ira D. Wallach Division of Art, Prints and Photographs: Print Collection, New York Public Library)

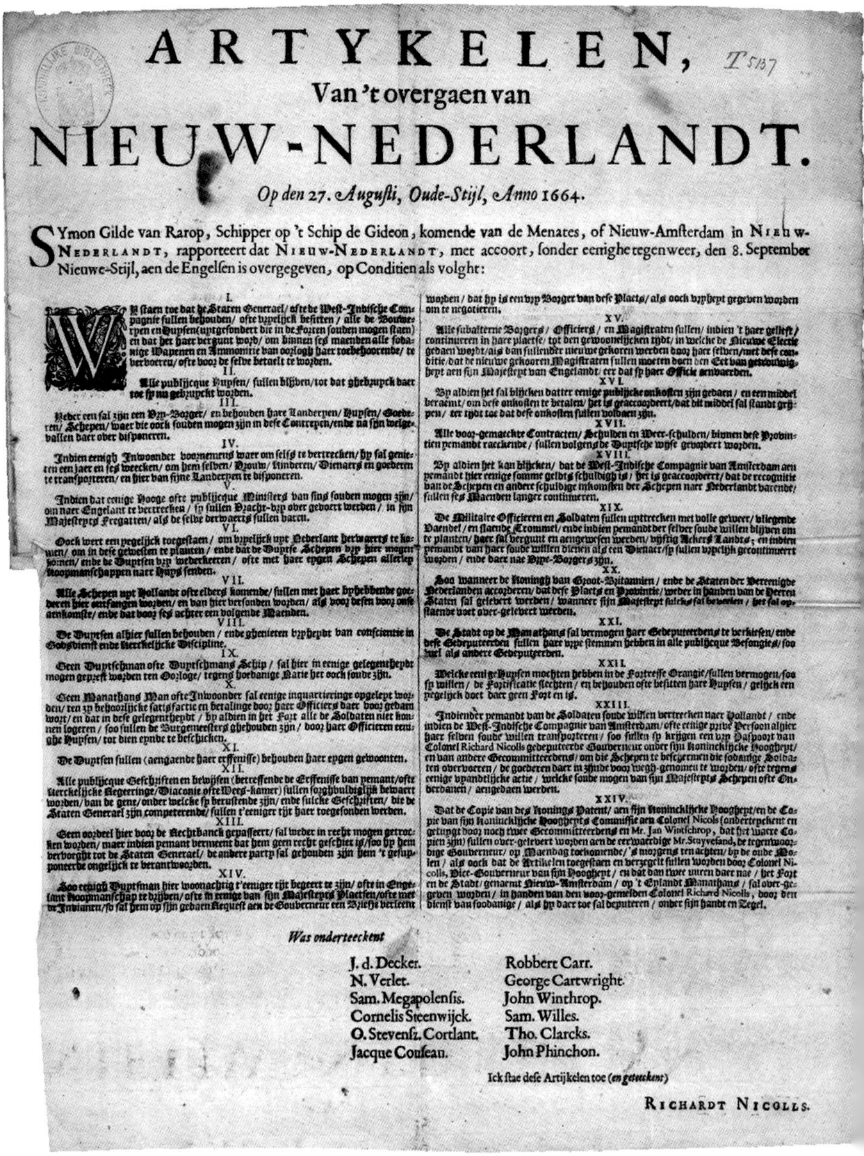

ARTYKELEN,

Van 't overgaen van

NIEUW-NEDERLANDT.

Op den 27. Augusti, Oude-Stijl, Anno 1664.

SYmon Gilde van Rarop, Schipper op 't Schip de Gideon, komende van de Menates, of Nieuw-Amsterdam in Nieuw-Nederlandt, rapporteert dat Nieuw-Nederlandt, met accoort, sonder eenighe tegenweer, den 8. September Nieuwe-Stijl, aen de Engelsen is overgegeven, op Conditien als volght:

Was onderteeckent

J. d. Decker. | Robbert Carr.
N. Verlet. | George Cartwright.
Sam. Megapolensis. | John Winthrop.
Cornelis Steenwijck. | Sam. Willes.
O. Stevensz. Cortlant. | Tho. Clarcks.
Jacque Cousseau. | John Phinchon.

Ick stae dese Artijkelen toe (*en geteeckent*)

RICHARDT NICOLLS.

The Articles of the Transfer of New Netherland, signed by Colonel Nicolls, allowed for much of the way of life of the Dutch colony to remain in place under British rule. Included was the right to "enjoy the liberty of their consciences in Divine Worship and church discipline"—in other words, a religious freedom clause.

New Amsterdam

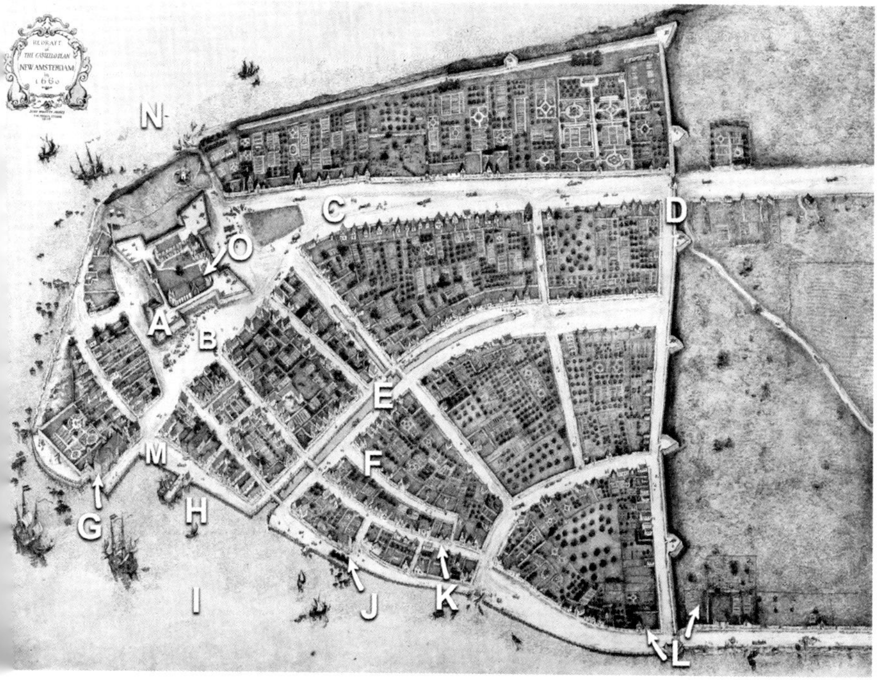

Redraft of the Castello Plan, *1916* (The Miriam and Ira D. Wallach Division of Art, Prints and Photographs: Print Collection, New York Public Library)

A—Fort
B—Market field
C—Broadway (Heere Street)
D—Wall
E—Canal
F—Possible street of first synagogue
G—Stuyvesant's home
H—Dock
I—East River
J—Stadthuys
K—Asser Levy's house in 1662
L—Approximate area of Levy's butcher shop
M—Pearl Street
N—North River (Hudson)
O—Dutch Reformed church

Author's Note

The story of the twenty-three Jews from Recife in New York is one that many Brazilians are proud to know. Unfortunately, most Americans are not familiar with this bit of history. Being Jewish and from Brazil, I too was told the tale of their exodus from Recife, the perilous journey, the pirate attack, the lawsuits, and the auction. I listened with pride about the "Brazilians" who "founded" the Jewish community of New York, as we love to boast about in my country.

But as I researched the documents, academic papers, books, and other historical evidence, I realized that several segments of the story are shrouded in mystery. Historians have questions about the exact path the *Falcon* took after leaving Recife. How many of the passengers were taken prisoner in Jamaica, and how many were released? Where exactly did the passengers meet Capt. Jacques de La Motthe? Did their arrival in New Amsterdam happen completely by chance? Or was it their intended destination when they fled? What exactly happened to the passengers after they arrived in

America? And one of the most important questions is whether Asser Levy arrived on the *St. Catherine,* or a couple of weeks earlier, on the *Pear Tree* from Amsterdam.

Unfortunately, the pieces of this nearly 400-year-old historical puzzle tell a choppy story. After reviewing all the data and interviewing many American, Dutch, and Brazilian experts on the subject, I believe that the story I have outlined is viable. It is, of course, a work of historical fiction. I have taken the liberty of filling in Asser Levy's character, based on his historical footprints. The narratives and scene descriptions are my vision of what the passengers may have encountered. Though many of the diary dates correspond accurately to the historical events, I have altered some of them for the fluidity of the story. The timeline I include contains all the dates verified by primary sources.

One thing, however, did become very clear to me as I was writing this book. Initially, I saw this as an account of the first large group of Jews who arrived in America, the hardships they endured, and the rights they won. But as I progressed, I noticed how much more universal and current this story is. Today, the world is experiencing a refugee crisis of epic proportions. I realized how, in fact, very little has changed over the centuries since this story took place. Millions of people today still must leave behind everything they know and own in their beloved homelands in order to escape religious persecution, war, and famine. Every day, families risk their lives on dangerous journeys. Many perish. Those who survive arrive at the doorstep of other countries much like the twenty-three passengers who arrived in New Amsterdam: homeless, poor, and hungry. They humbly seek an opportunity to work hard and be free to be themselves.

To Stuyvesant, the arrival of twenty-three penniless refugees in his colony of under 1,000 people may have felt the same as it would to the mayor of New York today if about 48,000 refugees arrived on a single day in Manhattan. Governments during any period in history worry about providing for refugees, how they will contribute to the society, how they will learn the language, and what impact their religion will have on their country.

America was founded by immigrants fleeing religious persecution. Yet many of the early English settlements did not allow religious diversity. New Amsterdam was not such a place. It inherited the concept of tolerance (almost unheard of at the time) from the Dutch. It was a cultural melting pot from the get-go. Since the arrival of the twenty-three passengers in 1654, New York has been the entry point for millions of refugees from around the world. Each of these cultures has fought for its space and rights and left its mark on our society.

Today, New York, with its 8.5 million inhabitants, still carries the legacy that the citizens of New Amsterdam created and the British embraced. It is the center of freedom and opportunity in the world, the symbol of the American dream.

Asser Levy's Mysterious Origins

Historians disagree about which ship brought Asser Levy to New Amsterdam: the *St. Catherine* or the *Pear Tree*. The court documents of New Netherland do give us some idea of who he was, what he did, and where he was on specific dates. They provide us with clues, like dots that can be connected. But historians have different ways of connecting those dots. Perhaps you can be a historical detective and create your own theory about Asser Levy's arrival in New Amsterdam.

Clues

- Asser Levy was an Ashkenazi (Eastern European) Jew. Though most Jews in the Brazilian colony were Portuguese Jews (Sephardic), some were Ashkenazi.
- Historians are not certain where Levy was from. He signed one document as being "from Swellem" (perhaps Schwelm in modern-day Germany). In another document, he appears as Aster Wilde, son of Judah Leib of Vilna, Poland.

- Many Eastern European Jews immigrated to Amsterdam in the mid-seventeenth century.
- Asser Levy's name is not signed in Recife's synagogue books.
- Benjamin Levy was the kosher butcher of Recife, from 1648 until 1654. He was old enough to be Asser's father, but it is not certain he was. Sons usually learned to be kosher butchers from their fathers.
- Asser became the first kosher butcher in America in 1678.
- The *Pear Tree* left Amsterdam on July 8, 1654, for London. It then sailed to New Amsterdam, arriving around August 22, 1654. Solomon Pietersen and Jacob Barsimon were Jews on that ship.
- Documents state that "some" Jewish traders were on the *Pear Tree*. If there were more than two, perhaps Levy was on it instead of the *St. Catherine.*
- The *Falcon* left Recife in February 1654 and landed unintentionally in Jamaica, which is in the West Indies.
- In early September 1654, the *St. Catherine* arrived with twenty-three Jewish refugees. Most if not all came from Brazil, but some may have been picked up along the way, perhaps in Jamaica. Domine Johannes Polhemius, who was the pastor in Brazil, was on the same ship.
- Jacques de La Motthe, the captain of the *St. Catherine,* sued the twenty-three Jews

for the fare from Cape St. Anthony, in the West Indies.

- Some of the *St. Catherine*'s passengers were Ricke (a lady, with perhaps an alternative spelling for Raicha or Rachel) Nounes, Judicq (Judith) De Mereda, Abram Israel, David Israel, and Moses Ambrosius.
- On September 14, 1654, Levy sued Mrs. Nounes to collect a loan he made to her and her husband in a place called "Gamonikę." This may be a misspelling of "Jamaique" (French for Jamaica), but no one knows for sure.
- Mrs. Nounes countersued Levy for money she lent him for his freight from the West Indies.
- On October 5, 1654, La Motthe sued Levy for 106 guilders still owed to him for the fare. Levy claimed he agreed to pay the captain his debt on the condition that his goods would not be auctioned. Since his goods were sold at auction, he claimed to be released from the debt.
- Levy seemed to distinguish himself from the other refugees with his many business skills.
- Levy seemed to be the only Jew among the first to arrive who made New Amsterdam his permanent home.

Historical Sites from This Story

Kahal Zur Israel Synagogue
Rua do Bom Jesus, 197, Recife, Brazil
The museum houses the ruins of the original synagogue, built in 1636 and considered the oldest synagogue in the New World. The twenty-three passengers would have attended religious services there. (Photograph by Daniela Weil)

Congregation Shearith Israel
2 West 70th Street, New York, New York
This is the congregation's fifth building. Though it was constructed in 1897, the congregation it houses was established by the twenty-three passengers upon their arrival in 1654. (Photograph by Daniela Weil)

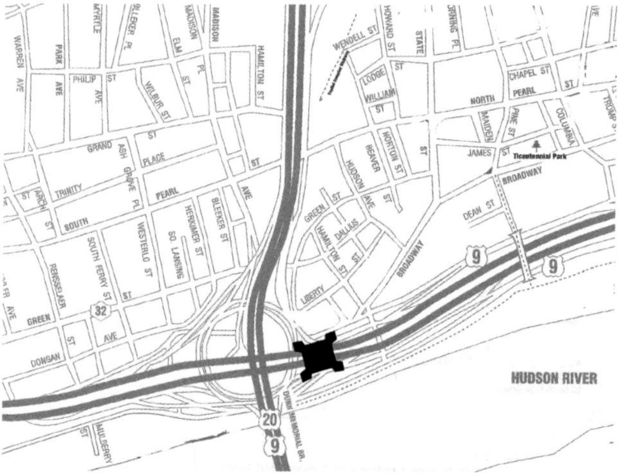

Fort Orange
The location of the fort that gave rise to the city of Albany is now under a large freeway intersection. The exact spot is in the north part of the circular loop where Interstate 787 meets Market Street.

Stuyvesant Square
2nd Avenue and 15th Street, New York, New York
A statue honors Petrus Stuyvesant. (Photograph by Daniela Weil)

Chatham Square Cemetery
55 St. James Place, New York, New York
This cemetery is the second oldest in New York, occupying land purchased in 1682. The tomb of Benjamin Bueno de Mesquita (1683) is the oldest Jewish grave in the city. He was a Portuguese Jew who fled Recife in 1654. (Photograph by Daniela Weil)

Stadthuys (City Hall)
Pearl Street and Coenties Alley, New York, NY
The outline of cream-colored bricks on the ground marks the spot where the Stadthuys or city hall stood. Built in 1641, it was where all of the court cases in this story took place. The adjacent bronze railings reveal excavations that have unearthed some of the original foundations. (Photograph by Daniela Weil)

Stone Street Historic District
Stone Street between Hanover Square and Coenties Alley, New York, New York
Asser Levy's house was located at the corner of Stone Street and Mill Lane. (Photograph by Daniela Weil)

St. Mark's Church in-the-Bowery
131 East 10th Street, New York, New York
This church marks the spot where a chapel once stood on Stuyvesant's farm in the Bowery. A plaque at the side of this building reads: In the Vault lies buried PETRUS STUYVESANT late Captain General and Governor in Chief of Amsterdam in New Netherland now called New York and the Dutch West India Islands, died Feb'y A.D. 1672 aged 80 years. (Photograph by Daniela Weil)

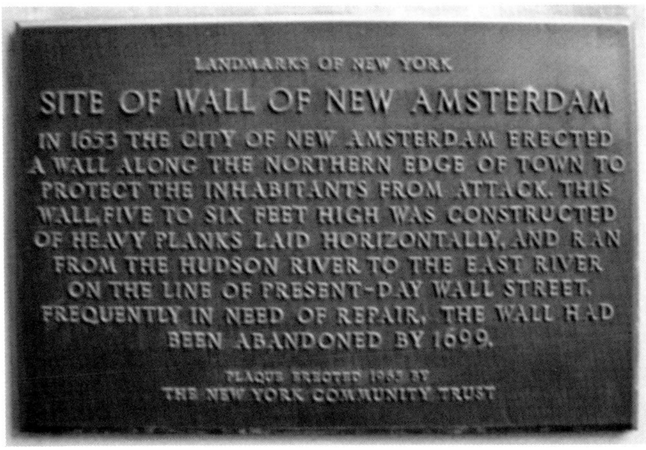

Wall Street Pavers
Wall Street, between Broadway and William Street, New York, New York
A series of pavers embedded in the cobblestones of Wall Street (formerly known as Het Cingel*) marks the location of New Amsterdam's Wall.*

Fort Christina
Fort Christina Park, Wilmington, Delaware
A monument has been built to honor the Swedish stronghold, which the Dutch took over in 1655.

Timeline

March 1623—The Dutch West India Company (WIC) sends first settlers to New Amsterdam.

March 3, 1630—The WIC takes over the town of Recife, in Brazil, from the Portuguese.

1636—Construction begins for Kahal Zur Israel Synagogue in Recife. It is the oldest Jewish congregation in the New World.

1647—Petrus Stuyvesant arrives in New Amsterdam, to become New Netherland's director-general.

January 26, 1654—The Portuguese Army recaptures Recife and gives the Dutch three months to leave.

February 24, 1654—The *Falcon* leaves the port of Recife.

Around April 1654—The *Falcon* docks in Jamaica. The Spanish take several Jews as prisoners.

Around August 1654—Capt. Jacques de La Motthe sails the *St. Catherine* from Cape St. Anthony, Cuba, heading for New Amsterdam.

August 22, 1654—The *Pear Tree* arrives in New Amsterdam from Holland with Jacob Barsimon and Solomon Pietersen.

September 7, 1654—La Motthe appears in court, claiming he is owed a balance of about 1,400 guilders for the passage of the twenty-three Jews he brought on the *St. Catherine*.

September 9, 1654—La Motthe goes to court again, asking permission to sell all of the passengers' belongings. The court gives the passengers four extra days to pay the captain.

September 12, 1654—The first Rosh Hashanah (Jewish New Year) service in New Amsterdam takes place.

September 13, 1654—La Motthe auctions off all the Jews' belongings.

September 16, 1654—The court gives La Motthe permission to take David Israel and Moses Ambrosius as prisoners until the passengers make the payment.

September 22, 1654—Stuyvesant sends a letter to the WIC, demanding that the Jews be expelled from New Amsterdam.

October 12, 1654—The court orders La Motthe to pay the cost of keeping the two Jewish prisoners, as well as extra sessions in court.

October 26, 1654—La Motthe agrees to transfer his debt to his crew and releases the Jews from his lawsuit.

November 14, 1654—The Dutch government writes a letter to the king of Spain demanding immediate release of Jewish prisoners in Jamaica.

January 1655—The New Amsterdam Jews send a petition to the WIC requesting the same rights as the Dutch citizens.

March 1, 1655—The court sues Abraham de la Simon, a Jew, for keeping his store open on a Sunday (the Christian sabbath). He is fined 600 guilders.

March 18, 1655—Domine Megapolensis writes a letter demanding that Jews be banished from the colony.

April 26, 1655—The WIC writes a letter that guarantees the Jews the right to remain in New Amsterdam and to travel freely and trade in New Netherland.

July 1655—The court denies a petition to allow a Jewish cemetery in New Amsterdam.

August 28, 1655—Stuyvesant denies Jewish men the civil right to stand guard at the Wall and help protect the colony from its enemies. In addition, he taxes them for not being able to serve.

September 11-15, 1655—Stuyvesant captures Fort Christina. New Sweden surrenders.

September 15, 1655—The Susquehannock Nation and allied Native Americans attack New Amsterdam and several New Netherland settlements along the Hudson River.

October 30, 1655—Stuyvesant states that Jews should not have the same liberties as other Dutch citizens, for fear of attracting more minority groups to the colony.

November 5, 1655—Asser Levy and Jacob Barsimon petition for their right to stand guard or not be taxed. The court denies the petition and suggests that they leave the colony instead.

November 29, 1655—Jews notify the WIC that they are still denied the right to travel, reside, and trade in the New Netherland territory.

December 23, 1655—The court denies the Jew Salvador D'andrada the right to buy a house in New Amsterdam.

February 22, 1656—The court grants the Jewish community the right to build a Jewish cemetery.

March 14, 1656—Jews send a letter of protest about Stuyvesant to the WIC.

June 14, 1656—The WIC writes Stuyvesant a letter reprimanding him for not allowing the Jews the same privileges of trade and freedom as other citizens. The WIC gives them the right to build houses, as long as they are grouped in a separate part of town, but not to practice their religion in public.

April 11, 1657—Levy petitions for **burgher rights.**

April 21, 1657—The court grants Levy burgher rights.

June 3, 1658—Barsimon is pardoned for not showing up in court on Saturday, the Jewish sabbath. This is the first sign of religious tolerance from the New Amsterdam court.

October 15, 1660—The court grants Levy a license to be a butcher. The city exempts him from having to slaughter pigs.

June 8, 1662—Levy purchases a house on Stone Street, becoming the first Jewish landowner in North America.

August 1664—Four British warships commanded by Col. Richard Nicolls surround New Amsterdam.

September 6, 1664—The Dutch and British sign the Articles of the Transfer of New Netherland. Nicolls becomes the first governor of New York.

October 21-26, 1664—Levy signs an oath of allegiance to the British Crown.

October 1665—Stuyvesant returns to Holland.

October 1667—Stuyvesant returns to New York. He lives the rest of his life on his farm in the Bowery.

February 1672—Stuyvesant dies near New York City. He is buried at the location of St. Mark's Church in-the-Bowery.

February 1, 1682—Levy dies in New York.

1683—Benjamin Bueno de Mesquita, a Portuguese Jew from Recife, dies and is buried in the oldest known Jewish grave in New York City.

1730—The court grants the Jewish community the right to build a synagogue. Congregation Shearith Israel is built on Mill Street (now South William Street).

Glossary

allez. "Let's go" or "come on" in French.

Amsterdam. The capital city of the Netherlands.

bar mitzvah. A Jewish rite of passage performed by boys when they turn thirteen.

Bohemia. A region in the modern-day Czech Republic.

Bowery. From the Dutch word *bouwerij,* a large farm. Today a neighborhood in New York City, it was the site of Stuyvesant's farm after the English takeover.

burgher. A full citizen of the Netherlands.

burgher rights. Citizens with burgher rights could travel freely inside Dutch territory, own homes, conduct business, run for office, and serve in the militia.

caravel. A small, highly maneuverable sailing ship developed in the fifteenth century by the Portuguese and used for exploration.

chuppah (HUH-pah). A canopy beneath which Jewish marriage ceremonies are performed.

director-general. The official title held by Petrus Stuyvesant as the governor of New Netherland.

Domine. The title given to an ordained minister of the Dutch Reformed Church.

Dutch. The name given to people from Holland or the Netherlands.

Dutch Reformed. A branch of Protestant Christianity that followed the teachings of John Calvin.

Dutch West India Company. Also known as the WIC, it was one of the largest trading companies in the world in the seventeenth century. It made fortunes by bringing goods such as sugar, wood, and fur from the Americas and selling them in Europe. It also traded slaves. The WIC conquered territories, ran the colonies, chose their officials, and paid their salaries. It also sent arms for protection and made all the laws and decisions concerning the colonies. Many of the shareholders (investors) of the WIC were Portuguese Jews in Amsterdam.

East River. A waterway that connects Upper New York Bay on its south end to Long Island Sound on its north end. It is not a river but a saltwater tidal estuary.

frigate. A common type of battleship used in the seventeenth century.

goedemorgen. "Good morning" in Dutch.

guilder. The currency of the Netherlands from the seventeenth century until 2002, when the euro came into use.

Heere Street. Known as Broadway today, Heere Street led from the fort to the Wall.

heretic. A Jew who had converted to Christianity but either reverted to Judaism or practiced Judaism secretly.

Inquisition. A religious court that began in the fifteenth century under King Ferdinand and Queen Isabella of Spain. Its mission was to find and punish anyone living in Spanish territory who was not Catholic. Suspects were arrested and questioned using torture. During this period, thousands of Jews and Muslims had to convert to Christianity or flee, under penalty of death. Protestants were also targeted.

interest. An extra amount of money charged for the privilege of borrowing money.

Jewish New Year. Also known as Rosh Hashanah (Rosh Hah-SHAH-nah), it is considered a "High Holy Day," one of the holiest days in Judaism. It is celebrated according to the lunar calendar, usually in the month of September. It is marked by the blowing of the shofar.

kosher. The Jewish dietary laws, which describe how an animal must be slaughtered. Certain types of meat, such as pork, are not allowed to be consumed.

mazel tov. "Congratulations" or "good luck" in Yiddish or Hebrew.

minyan. A quorum of ten people over the age of thirteen required for traditional Jewish public worship.

Nassau. Johan Maurits van Nassau was a Dutch prince and governor of Dutch Brazil from 1637 to 1644. He is known for building a planned city on an island across from Recife. It boasted a palace, roads, canals, and gardens in the Dutch style and was aptly named Mauritsstad. He also built the first bridge connecting the island to the mainland, which still stands today.

Netherlands. A kingdom in Western Europe bordering Germany and Belgium, composed of twelve provinces (similar to states). The two most populated and developed provinces are North and South Holland. The term *Holland* is often used to refer to the Netherlands as a whole.

New France. The area colonized by France in North America. Part of that territory became modern-day Canada.

New Sweden. A Swedish colony that existed along the Delaware River (in the present-day states of Delaware, New Jersey, and Pennsylvania) from 1638 to 1655. Their main settlement was Fort Christina, which Stuyvesant took over in August 1655.

North River. In the seventeenth century, the Hudson River was known as the North River. It was the waterway taken to reach Fort Orange (Albany) and other towns in New Netherland.

odyssey. A long journey, filled with adventures and challenges. The epic poem *The Odyssey,* by Homer, described the journey taken by the Greek mythical hero Odysseus.

pantofles. High-heeled slippers.

Pearl Street. One of the oldest streets in New York. It followed the shoreline of the East River in New Amsterdam and was named for the abundance of oyster shells at the water's edge, some of which lined the surface of the road.

rabbi. A preacher, usually the leader of a congregation, who studies and teaches Jewish law.

red flag. In the seventeenth century, buccaneer ships in the Caribbean flew red flags. Buccaneers were pirates who often attacked Spanish ships carrying gold from Central America to Europe. The flag symbolized the bloodshed that would ensue if the target ship did not surrender peacefully.

refugees. People who are looking for a new place to settle because they have had to escape war, persecution, or natural disasters in their home country.

shochet (shaw-HET). A Jew who has been trained to be a kosher butcher. Benjamin Levy was the shochet of Recife until 1653, when he was taken off the payroll.

shofar. A ram's-horn trumpet used by Jews during the New Year service.

South River. In the seventeenth century, the Delaware River was called the South River. It was a major Indian fur-trading route.

Stadthuys (STAHT-hayz). Originally built as a tavern, the "State House" was the city hall of New Amsterdam. In its courtroom, all matters ranging from squabbles between neighbors to important political questions were settled.

stepped gables. A stair-step type of design

at the top of the triangular roof end of a building. It is typical of Dutch architecture.

synagogue. A Jewish temple of worship.

Tahte. "Father" or "Dad" in Yiddish.

tallit. A fringed garment worn by Jewish males as a prayer shawl.

Torah. The holy scrolls that contain the sacred literature of the Jewish tradition. There is a Torah in all Jewish temples.

trainbands. A group of civilian soldiers put together for battle.

waistcoat. A vest or short jacket.

Wall. A fortified wall that protected New Amsterdam from attacks from the north. The Dutch referred to it as the palisades or works (fortification). The street that ran alongside it was known as *Het Cingel* (the belt). After the British took over, it became known as "Wall Street."

Wallonia. A region of Belgium with its own customs and language.

wampum. Traditional beads of the Native American tribes who lived along the North Atlantic coast. The beads were made from different types of clam shells found in the region and were widely used as currency during colonial times.

West Indies. The name given to the Caribbean islands during the age of exploration. Some territories in the northern part of South America, such as the Guianas, were also considered part of the West Indies.

Zeide. "Grandfather" in Yiddish.

Websites

The New Netherland Institute holds a wide array of documents, videos, maps, paintings, and references on the history of New Amsterdam: *www.newnetherlandinstitute.org.*

The New Amsterdam History Center website contains 3D tours, links, lesson plans, and information on the history of New Amsterdam. It includes a digital model of the house Asser Levy bought in 1662: *www.newamsterdamhistorycenter.org.*

This public media source contains videos, interactive documents such as the original Articles of the Transfer of New Netherland, and much information on the history of New Netherland: *www.thirteen.org/dutchny.*

The original petition by the Jews to the Dutch West India Company can be seen here: *http://digitalhistory.hsp.org/pafrm/doc/jewish-petition-dutch-west-india-company-january-1655.*

Len Tantillo is a painter who specializes in accurate depictions of the colony of New Netherland. Some of his work can be viewed at: *www.lftantillo.com.*

Congregation Shearith Israel, established by the twenty-three passengers in 1654, has a website with information on the history of its founding fathers: *www.shearithisrael.org.*

Kahal Zur Israel synagogue in Brazil is the oldest synagogue in the New World, and the website has information on its archeology and history: *www.kahalzurisrael.com/en.*

This interactive map of New Amsterdam contains the locations of Asser Levy's home and the Stadthuys: *www.ekamper.net.*

The sounds of New Netherland in the 1600s are recaptured by an audio/visual project named "Calling Thunder: the Unsung History of Manhattan": *www.unsung.nyc/#home.*

The New York Department of Records and Information Services has beautifully organized links to records and images related to New Amsterdam: *www.archives.nyc/newamsterdam/.*

Bibliography

Books and Articles

Arbell, Mordechai. *The Jewish Nation of the Caribbean: The Spanish-Portuguese Jewish Settlements in the Caribbean and the Guianas.* Jerusalem: Gefen, 2002.

Birmingham, Stephen. *The Grandees: America's Shephardic Elite.* New York: Harper & Row, 1971.

Daly, Charles P. *The Settlement of the Jews in North America.* New York: Philip Cowen, 1893.

Ferreira Miranda, B. R. "*Gente de guerra: Origem cotidiano e resistência dos soldados do exercito da companhia das Indias Ocidentais no Brasil (1630-1654)*." Ph.D. diss., Leiden University, 2011. https://openaccess.leidenuniv.nl/handle/1887/18047.

Ferreira Miranda, B. R., and Virgínia Maria Almoêdo de Assis. "*Fortes, paliçadas e redutos enquanto estrategia da política de defesa Portuguesa (o caso da capitania de Pernambuco 1654-1701)*." Master's thesis, Universidade Federal de Pernambuco, Recife, 2006.

Friedman, Lee. "The Petition of Jacques de La Motthe." *The Green Bag* 13 (1901): 396-98.

Gelfand, Noah. "Jews in New Netherland: An Atlantic Perspective." In *Explorers, Fortunes & Love Letters: A Window on New Netherland,* edited by Martha Dickinson Shattuck. Albany: New Netherland Institute, 2009.

Hershkowitz, Leo. "Asser Levy and the Inventories of Early New York Jews." *American Jewish History* 80 (1990-91): 21.

———. "By Chance or Choice: Jews in New Amsterdam 1654." *American Jewish Archives Journal* 57 (2005): 1-13.

———. "Some Aspects of the New York Jewish

Merchant and Community, 1654-1820." *American Jewish Historical Quarterly* 66 (1976-77): 10-34.

Jacobs, Jaap. "Not to Exclude the Jewish Nation, but to Allow Passage to and Residence in that Country: Jews in New Amsterdam." In *Joden in de Cariben*, edited by Julie-Marthe Cohen, 74-85. Zutphen, Netherlands: WalburgPers, 2015.

Kritzler, Edward. *Jewish Pirates: How a Generation of Swashbuckling Jews Carved Out an Empire in the New World in Their Quest for Treasure, Religious Freedom—and Revenge*. New York: Doubleday, 2008.

Ladurie, Emmanuel Le Roy. Times of Feast, Times of Famine: A History of Climate Since the Year 1000. Garden City, NY: Doubleday, 1971.

Oppenheim, Samuel. "The Early History of the Jews in New York, 1654-1664." *American Jewish Historical Quarterly* 18 (1909): 1-91.

———. "More about Jacob Barsimson." *American Jewish Historical Society* (1925): 39-51.

———. "The Question of the Kosher Meat Supply in New York in 1818: With a Sketch of Early Conditions." *American Jewish Historical Society* 25 (1917): 21-62.

Paravazian, Diane. "Globalization and Languages in New York City: A Case Study." Globalization101.org.

Pool, David De Sola. *Portraits Etched in Stone*. New York: Columbia University Press, 1952.

Schappes, Morris U. *A Documentary History of the Jews in the United States 1654-1875*. 1950. Reprint, New York: Schocken Books, 1971.

Stern, Malcolm. "Asser Levy—A New Look at Our Jewish Founding Father." *American Jewish Archives Journal* 26 (1974): 66-77.

Tertre, Jean-Baptiste du. *Histoire gęnęrale des Antilles*. Paris, 1667.

Vainfas, Ronaldo. *Jerusalęm Colonial: Judeus Portugueses no Brasil Holandês*. Civilização Brasileira, 2010.

Valentine, D. "Manual of the Corporation of the City of New York." *New York (N.Y.). Common Council* (1865): 691, 701.

Varnhagen, Francisco Adolfo de. *Historia do Brasil: Antes da sua separaçao e independencia de Portugal*. Rio de Janeiro: Laemmert, 1870.

Wainer, Ann Helen. *Jewish and Brazilian Connections to New York, India, and Ecology: A Collection of Essays.* Privately printed, 2012.

Weitman, David, and Marco Maciel. *Bandeirantes espirituais do Brasil: Rabinos Isaac Aboab da Fonseca e Mosseh Rephael d'Aguilar, sęculo XVII.* São Paulo: Maayanot, 2003.

Wiznitzer, Arnold. "The Exodus from Brazil and Arrival in New Amsterdam of the Jewish Pilgrim Fathers, 1654." *American Jewish Historical Society* 44 (1954): 80-97.

———. *Jews in Colonial Brazil.* New York: Columbia University Press, 1960.

———. "The Number of Jews in Dutch Brazil." *Jewish Social Studies* (1954): 106-14.

———. *The Records of the Earliest Jewish Community in the New World.* New York: American Jewish Historical Society, 1954.

Wolff, Egon, and Frieda Wolff. *Dicionario biografico.* Rio de Janeiro: ERCA, 1986.

———. "Mistaken Identities of Signatories of the Congregation Zur Israel, Recife." *Studia Rosenthaliana* 12 (1978): 91-107.

———. "The Problem of the First Jewish Settlers in New Amsterdam, 1654." *Studia Rosenthaliana* 15 (1981): 169-77.

Documents

Amsterdam City Archives.

"Articles of Capitulation on the Reduction of New Netherland." Secretary of State's Office, Albany: General Entries, I., 1664-1665, p. 23.

Barreto, Francisco. Dutch text of letter to Supreme Council, April 8, 1654. Oppenheim Collection. American Jewish Historical Society, Boston.

Brodhead, John Romeyn, Berthold Fernow, and E. B. O'Callaghan. *Documents Relative to the Colonial History of the State of New-York: Procured in Holland, England, and France.* Vol. 3. Albany: Weed, Parsons, 1853.

Fernow, Berthold. *The Records of New Amsterdam: Minutes of the Court of Burgomasters and Schepens 1653-1655.* New York: Knickerbocker, 1897.

Gehring, Charles T., trans. and ed. *Council Minutes, 1655-1656.* New Netherland Documents Series. Syracuse: Syracuse University Press, 1995.

———. *Laws & Writs of Appeal 1647-1663.* New Netherland Documents Series. Syracuse: Syracuse University Press, 1991.

Hastings, Hugh. *Ecclesiastical Records: State of New York.* Vol. 1. Albany: J. B. Lyon, 1901.

"Index to the Public Record of the County of Albany, State of New York 1630-1894." *Publications of the American Jewish Historical Society* 26: 247.

Mercator, Gerard. *Atlas Minor.* Amsterdam: Jansson, 1630.

Minutes of th High and Secret Councils of Brazil, Governor and Councils of Brazil, and High Government of Brazil.

Mortera, Saul Levi. "Providencia de dios con Ysrael" (ca. 1654-60). Transcribed, translated, and introduction by Gregory B. Kaplan. Ets Haim Library, Amsterdam.

National Archive, The Hague.

O'Callaghan, E. B. *Calendar of Historical Manuscripts in the Office of the Secretary of State Albany.* Albany, 1865.

"Powers of Attorney, Acknowledgments, Indentures of Apprenticeship, Inventories, Deeds, &c., 1651-1656." Office of City Clerk, New York.

"Whereupon . . . New Netherlands Were Surrendered, September 29, 1664." True copy of articles. Gilder Lehrman Collection, New York.

Videos

Mesel, Katia. *The Rock and the Star [O Rochedo e a Estrela].* Arrecife Produções, 2011. Documentary film.

REDRAFT
of
THE CASTELLO PLAN
NEW AMSTERDAM
in
1660